THE MUSE OF WALLACE ROSE

Novella and Short Stories

Bill Woods

WESTVIEW
Kingston Springs, Tennessee

Prepared by Westview for publication at Ingram Spark.
P.O. Box 605
Kingston Springs, TN 37082
www.publishedbywestview.com

ISBN 978-1-62880-180-4 Perfect bound
ISBN 978-1-62880-181-1 Amazon Kindle
ISBN 978-1-62880-182-8 Smashwords

First edition, May 2019

Acknowledgments

Thanks to my Harpeth River Writer friends.
Any good passages are likely the result of their rough stewardship.
A special thanks to Pat Spencer for editing.

Disclaimer

Likeness of these characters to any real persons
is accidental on my part,
and paranoia on your part.

This is a work of fiction.
Any truth contained herein, I'll swear never happened.

Table of Contents

Prologue.. 1

The Muse of Wallace Rose............................. 3

Catalpa Trees... 145

The Widow's Tale...................................... 155

Buster 159

Million Dollar Baby.................................... 171

The Christmas Present................................. 179

The Snake God 185

The Lesson 191

An Alternate Reality 195

Gallup.. 201

Lady Macbeth... 205

Crystalina.. 215

Lighthouse Mission 223

The List.. 229

Grand Canyon... 241

The Collector 243

Prologue

Restless Dead People

Journal entry 03/05/2016:

2:30 AM - Awakened by another story, or rather a scene. I never get a whole story. Lay awake for an hour trying to make sense of it. Then, what the hell, might as well get up, put something on paper. Afterwards, maybe I can sleep again.

4:00 AM - Made coffee. Guess I'm up for the duration. What a life.

It's like dead people (their souls still alive) do this to me. "Get up! Tell my story!" When I sleep, I must be close to wherever dead people go.

It's never words, just images and emotions. Maybe that's where a writer comes in—giving voice to restless dead people. If I write their story well, they leave me alone. If I don't write, or write poorly, they haunt me.

I hope to do this to somebody when I'm dead.

The Muse of Wallace Rose

Chapter 1

He can make people do anything he wants. He can make them screw each other, or screw over each other. If they don't please him, he just kills them off. And he does sometimes, just for the fun of it. No appeal on their part; no remorse on his part.

That's why Wallace knows the blonde at the table in the back corner is gonna die. That's his table. Everybody at the café knows that's his table. Being new is no excuse. No bullet-in-the-brain quick death for her. She'll have to suffer.

He pulls out a chair at the next to last table and is sitting with his back to her thinking up nasty tortures when this guy pushes through the swinging glass door. He stops and checks out everybody in the joint; there are only Wallace and the blonde and two town slackers sitting at the counter gabbing with Vera, the waitress. He's wearing loafers with no socks and a tight-fitting white turtleneck to show off his muscles. When he coolly saunters past to the woman's table, Wallace scrunches his nose at the waft of Old Spice.

Vera brings over Wallace's usual breakfast and then turns to them.

"Two black coffees; one check," the man says.

He's got one of those commanding voices. Wallace can't eyeball them, but what they say is plain enough. Neither talks again until after Vera brings their coffee.

"Tonight," the guy says. She doesn't reply. "Is there any reason we shouldn't do it tonight?" She still doesn't answer. "Look, I know you're scared. But we've talked about it enough. We've decided to do it, haven't we?"

Wallace hears her shush him, the faint sound of air being let out of a tire, and then he can only hear bits and pieces. "Naked … bedroom." It doesn't take an Einstein to figure out what they're up to, but their hush-hush blows Wallace's fuses.

"You're mine too, Bub," Wallace mouths to himself through clenched teeth. Maybe the guy's just lining up a piece of ass, but there'll be another surprise waiting. Maybe she'll be one of those hermaphrodites. Wallace catches himself chuckling and glances to see if Vera heard. She's eyeing him with a stern control-yourself look.

The couple talks even quieter, but Wallace doesn't need to hear more to imagine what comes next:

> *"I wish we could do it now," she'd say.*
> *"Now?"*
> *"Hmm …" she'd purr with a seductive smile.*
> *"Follow me in three minutes," he'd say pushing back from the table. He'd scoot sideways past the ice machine to the tiny bathroom in the back. The woman would wait until the cook is turned to the griddle and then she'd go back there too. They'd do it with their clothes pushed aside, with her back against a wall. He'd put his hand over her mouth when she starts to moan. "It was the best I ever had," he'd say when it was over.*

Maybe they get caught. Wallace grins thinking about the two old men at the counter pointing and laughing. Maybe Vera threatens to call the cops. When he imagines the blonde bawling as she runs out the door, a cackle slips out. Vera, the bitch, gives him the look again.

He doesn't have to hang around this crummy café to make stuff happen. It can wait until he gets back to the apartment, to his writing desk. Wallace waves a five-spot for Vera to see, then slips it under his coffee cup. "Keep the change," he retorts to her scowl. A quarter tip is all she deserves.

When he gets up to leave, he glances back to freeze the couple's images in his mind for use later. They're gone. He ambles back to the bathroom and tries the handle. It's locked.

Chapter 2

At the corner, Wallace leans against the red brick wall of a travel agency. The guy comes out first and walks away toward the far end of the street. She comes out a minute later and turns in Wallace's direction. He studies the vacation packages displayed in the window as she walks past.

After she crosses at the corner to the other side of the street, he follows. From her backside, Wallace can understand the guy's interest in her. She has a bubble ass you rarely see on a white woman. The high heels and tight skirt advertise it to perfection. It screams—*if you've got the money, Honey*—. But he can tell by the tailored clothes, she ain't cheap. She's too classy for this part of town, too refined to be doing it in the toilet of a two-bit café. She's slumming.

She turns in at a hardware store in the middle of the block. When Wallace walks by the glass front, the clerk at the checkout counter is pointing to the back of the store, giving her directions. When she strides out of sight, he goes in and starts looking through the bin of "$5.99 or less" tools in the main aisle. He's got this set of Chinese screwdrivers in front of his face when she comes back with a roll of duct tape.

While waiting for another customer at the checkout, she places the tape on the counter and a credit card on top. The man in line in front of her turns to the side and shakes his head. It's him, the guy from the café. She puts the card back in her wallet and pulls out some bills instead. The clerk sacks a claw hammer for the man before ringing up her purchase. They leave separately without talking or even looking at the other.

Thinking about the couple, Wallace meanders in a daze to his studio above the dry cleaner. He flops on the couch and replays it all in his head. Yeah, them two doing it in the toilet right after he'd imagined it was just a coincidence. But they seemed to be following his thoughts like a script. What had tipped him off that they would do something so outlandish? He grinned with pride at the ceiling concluding it was his finely-honed writer's instinct that made reading people so easy.

And then there was that bit in the hardware store, them meeting and then acting like they didn't know each other. What was that all about? No way to know, but it was too good a scene to waste. He could use it later in one of his stories to add mystery and drama. You just can't make up good material like that.

Wallace turns on the laptop and tries to concentrate on his next story, but can't get the couple off his mind. Them two are plotting something. He can't figure it at first, and then he does. He names the blonde Denise and the man Stanley and starts writing. He'd think up a catchy title later.

Chapter 3

???????

By Wallace Rose

Denise had the cab drop her off at the corner of Dade and Charlotte. She immediately felt out of her element, conspicuous. The River City Diner sign hung over the sidewalk halfway down the block and she started that way. She was early, but it would be better to wait inside rather than risk being seen by somebody she knew driving by.

She hesitated in front of the glass door looking in and then walked past to the other end of the block. She couldn't go in that rat hole. She should phone for a taxi and get herself back to the shopping district where she belonged. But Stanley would never forgive her. He would be here in a few minutes. Thinking of Stanley's confident swagger brought her smile back and she returned to the café and went inside.

Wallace finishes writing the events of the morning. He rocks back in his swivel chair and reads it over, occasionally leaning forward to make a correction. It's a good start. He only had to embellish slightly to get his hooks in the reader. Now for a powerful ending.

He gets up and paces in front of the only window in his little apartment, massaging his right earlobe and staring blankly at the floor. Suddenly, he dashes back to the computer before his inspiration evaporates.

Denise, *standing in her pink panties at the upstairs bedroom window, watched Stanley emerge from the woods that separated the mansion from the street. He'd sneaked in to see her before and knew how to conceal himself from the security camera aimed at the driveway. The back door was unlocked.*

She waited, stretched across the bed on her back, as he meticulously draped his clothes on the back of her antique Queen Ann chair. They made love tenderly at first and then he was increasingly rough, digging his fingernails into her flesh. When he was through, he pulled her by her hands to stand in front of him. Before she could ask why, he punched her square in the mouth. She crumpled back onto the bed with a startled shriek. When she lowered her hands from her face, there were smears of blood on her fingers.

"It's got to look right, Babe. I'm sorry, but it's got to look real."

She clenched her eyes and grabbed a pillow to cover her face as her shoulders heaved.

"You understand, don't you Babe?"

He waited until her crying stopped. "Babe?"

She put the pillow aside and nodded her head.

"You're just gonna have to trust me from here on in. Listen closely and do exactly like I say. There's no backing out now. Understand?"

She sat up stiffly and looked him straight in the eyes and nodded again.

He fished in the pocket of the pants draped on the chair and pulled out a sandwich bag before walking into the master bathroom. He threw the condom he'd just used in the commode and flushed. As the bowl began to fill again, he dumped in another used condom from the sandwich bag. It settled to the bottom and was sucked partially into the drain. That condom came from the dumpster outside a whorehouse he sometimes visited.

"He used a rubber, see?" he yells into the bedroom "And you heard him flush it down the toilet. Can you remember that?

"How much time do we have?" He asked when he walked out.

Denise looked over at the alarm clock on the nightstand. "He always walks in at exactly five-thirty. Fifteen minutes."

"We've got to hurry then. Where's the duct tape?" She pointed to a hardware store bag in the chair seat. "Flip over." He gathered her arms behind her back and wrapped her wrists together. She looked over her shoulder in terror. "Don't worry, Babe. I've torn the tape almost in two. Just a little struggle and you'll be free. It's got to look right."

After taking the claw hammer out of the bag he'd brought, he stuffed both bags into his trousers pockets. Her eyes followed as he took his clothes to the bathroom, neatly stacking them on the counter. He walked back out closing the door behind him.

Flipping her onto her back, he lowered his face in front of hers. "Call him up here. Don't let on anything's wrong. Tell him you've got a surprise for him. See? You get the drift?"

She didn't answer. Her face was frozen like a corpse. He was about to rehearse with her what to say when they heard the front door slam. Her eyes got big. He held his trigger finger to his lips and backed behind the open door. They locked eyes, her lying naked on the bed with her arms behind her and him naked behind the door with the hammer arched over his head.

The shout came from downstairs, "Pet, are you home?"

The stairs squeaked s as Denise's husband came up. He stopped at the foot of the bed. Denise forced a smile at him but couldn't help letting her gaze shift to behind the door. The husband turned just in time for the claws of he hammer to bury in his forehead. The force of the blow knocked him to his knees, and then he crumpled forward. She screamed. Blood pooled at Stanley's feet and he stepped back.

After watching for a moment to see if the body moved, he looked at her cowering in a ball. She had pulled her arms free from the tape and a whine came from behind her hands. He'd have to cut his losses and kill her too if she couldn't pull this off.

He was considering it when she asked from behind her hands, "Are you sure he's dead?"

The blood had quit gushing, but the puddle of blood continued to grow. "Yeah, he's dead. Are you OK? Can you pull yourself together?" He tried to sound sympathetic until her whine turned into a wail. "Stop that blubbering!"

She lowered her hands and stared at him. She'd picked up on the threat in his voice.

"Just lie back. Don't look at him or you'll get sick. Don't do nothing till I get back."

He went into the bathroom and took a shower. He came out fully dressed, pushing a towel with the toe of his shoe to mop where he'd walked. Carefully stepping around the blood splatters, he wiped the handle of the hammer still stuck in the husband's *skull. He spread the towel at the door and wiped the soles of his shoes as he looked up at her lying quietly watching.*

"He was black, remember? And he had a stocking over his head." She nodded. "Say it," he demanded.

"Black—stocking over his head."

"You done good," he assured her. "It's all gonna be okay. Just got to get through the rest without a hitch, see?" She nodded. "We've talked it all through. There's nothing to worry about, see?" She nodded again and wiped at her eyes.

Stepping backward into the hall, he picked up the pink dappled towel and threw it onto the chair. Again he thought about killing her.

Denise shivered under his penetrating scowl. "I love you," she said with a weak smile.

"Love you too, Babe. Give me thirty minutes." He waved at the clock. "Then call 911. Those calls are recorded, so make it good." She nodded. "Don't call me, okay? I'll meet you at that diner in ten days. That's Friday after next. Ten o'clock."

They stared at each other.

"You're on your own now, Babe." He waited for her to nod and then he was gone.

She got up and pulled the bathrobe from the back of the bathroom door. The duct tape hung on the terrycloth fabric when she pushed her arms through. She scooted back across the bed rather than walk through the blood and stood at the window looking down. After Stanley melted back into the trees, she continued to survey the grounds, the Olympic pool, the Mercedes in the driveway. It was all hers now.

The End

Chapter 4

Wallace hits ENTER and looks at his wristwatch. Two hours. He'd blown right through it. A little cleanup and the story would be done.

He checks his emails and deletes the usual trash. An email from Josh promises payment soon. Well, "soon" better be really soon or he'd be sending his stuff elsewhere. Josh doesn't publish the only pulp mag out there.

The latest issue of *Suspense* lies on the desk beside the computer. The cover is a comic book style illustration of a busty girl with her arms thrown up to ward off a knife thrust by a tattooed arm coming from the edge of the page. He thumbs over to his story and stares at his name under the title. His writing's too good for this rag anyway. A story a month at ten cents a word just barely pays the rent. "I can do better," he mumbles.

He reads the new story through again from the beginning and corrects the errors caught by the word processor. He adds a title, "A Lovely Murder," and attaches the file to an email to Josh. The deadline for the next issue is the end of the week, then two weeks after that; he'd get a check. Funds were getting low, but he'd make it.

Wallace is surprised to have an email from Josh in the inbox the next morning. Yeah, Josh would accept the story, but according to him, it was below *Suspense*'s standards:

> **Wallace,**
> **The murder scene was OK, but the sex was flat. I didn't get a hard-on during the whole story. And you let the perps get away. You know how I hate that. It's immoral. How about a sequel**

and get this guy killed in a shootout with the cops?

But not before some juicy sex with the blonde. Bubble ass? Is that the best you can do? How about some more "nipples like Bakelite knobs on a toaster oven" (my personal favorite).

Josh

"PS: I wouldn't be so pushy if I didn't know you could do better, Ole Boy."

The son-of-a-bitch. How many ways can you spice up two people humping? It's all been done before. Well, they'll be doing it with donkeys next time, if that's what's selling.

When his little tizzy subsides, he pushes back in his chair and pulls at his earlobe. *A sequel?* Then it begins to grow. *Installments!* He could probably milk this for three or four—maybe 20,000 words total. He did the math quickly. $2000 bucks! That would be his biggest payday yet.

He pulls up a reply screen:

Send money now, you fag!

He holds down the delete key and starts over.

Josh,

This was the first installment of a series. The other three episodes are already written and include your splendid suggestions. Way ahead of you, Ole Boy. The total word count is 25,000.

If you agree, I'll send the rest of the installments before your next deadline.

Your compadre,
Wallace

He massages his earlobe before continuing.

PS: Please reply with your acceptance immediately since I have other offers.

Wallace gets up and stretches. He turns on the little TV he'd bought from Goodwill for twenty-five bucks. They didn't have the remote. A coat hanger sticks out the back as a makeshift antenna. As the TV warms up, he checks his watch to see if his favorite reality show is on yet. The tail end of a late-breaking news bulletin stops him before he can change channels.

The picture is the earnest face of that cute little reporter on Channel 6 holding a microphone in both hands to her mouth like a phallus. Behind her is a massive stone arch over a gated driveway.

" ... rape and murder. Police have confirmed that Citizen's Bank President Randolph Ballard is dead, apparently murdered when he returned home and discovered his wife being raped. His wife, Lucille Ballard, has been taken to Virgin Mother Hospital with non-life-threatening injuries. Further details are being withheld pending investigation. Back to you, Ron."

The studio anchor's face pops onto the screen. He introduces the weather lady.

Wallace switches channels. A midget is standing on a stool under a flower-studded arbor marrying this gorilla in a tuxedo. But Wallace can't get the image of the wrought iron gate, the semblance of security, off his mind. *Ain't nobody safe no more.* Tomorrow she'll be reporting a different murder, another on-the-scene report with as much gore in the background as the censors will allow. Most of the time it's one gangbanger killing another gangbanger—who cares, but not always. Rich folks think they can hide away in their walled-in estates, but those wrought iron gates just put a target on their backs. *Hey, this guy's got something worth protecting. Whatever it is, I want some.* That's how the criminal element thinks. He smiles before losing himself in the midget wedding. In his line of work, you get to be an expert on the criminal element.

Chapter 5

The next morning, precisely at ten, Wallace grabs the newspaper off the café's counter before heading back to his table. It's wrinkly and limp from all the greasy hands that had flipped through it already.

"Hey, Wally. How about pancakes this morning?" Vera greets cheerfully.

Bitch. He'd killed Vera so many times it wasn't even fun anymore. She knows he has the same thing every morning, and she knows he hates being called Wally. She's got that grin on her face, waiting for him to rise to the bait. He unfurls the paper in front of his face and gives it a snap. She'll bring his usual if he waits. *The bitch*.

One of the flunkies at the counter had pulled out the funnies, but the front page was there. Stretched across the top:

RANDOLPH BALLARD MURDERED, WIFE RAPED!!!

The police were looking for a black guy, five foot ten and stocky.

> **... if anyone saw a man fitting this description wearing dark blue overalls in the Highland neighborhood yesterday afternoon, call Crime stoppers ...**

That must be the wife's description. This stupid amateur deserves to get caught. Wallace Rose would never write a story where the rapist didn't kill the victim, the only witness. It's just not realistic. These thugs should read more.

At the bottom of the article:

**... Barnes Funeral Home is in charge
of arrangements.**

"Hey, Vera. Bring the phone book when you come. I mean, if you're gonna bring me coffee sometime this morning."

It had been a while since he'd been to a funeral. And this would be one of those high-dollar affairs. All his stories involved death, so he found himself writing about funerals frequently. *Got to keep up with my research.* At the least, he could watch some crying. He had a hard time writing the soppy stuff without an example to follow. Those heart-tugging details were always good filler to up the word count. Some readers even liked it.

He calls the funeral home on the payphone by the door and they have Ballard's funeral penciled in for Friday at two in the afternoon. There'd be a swarm of people there so nobody would notice him off to the side.

Chapter 6

It is still drizzling when the black limousine rolls up. The train of cars trailing behind with their headlights streaking through the mist is being directed into a parking lot at the bottom of the hill. The mourners would be soaked by the time they trudged to the gravesite. *Perfect!*

He stoops to place the bouquet of fresh lilies he'd found at another grave against the headstone in front of him—somebody's dear child who is "with the angels." He bows his head in mourning as he watches from under the brim of his rain hat.

Mister Randolph Ballard is conveniently already here; dry in a burnished nickel vault suspended above the grave on an Astroturf-covered platform. He must have been loaded out the back door of the church and whisked to the cemetery separately. Barnes probably thought trusting the casket to pallbearers in wet weather would be risky.

The driver of the limo and an attendant who had been riding shotgun get out in rain slickers and plastic covered hats. They stand ready as the rear passenger door opens. A patent leather pump feels for the ground and then there are long fishnet-covered legs with a black dress gathered halfway up the thighs. The driver holds a black umbrella as the woman stands. A dark veil flowing down from her wide brim hat covers her face. The attendant drapes a raincoat over her shoulders and the three of them walk to the front row of folding chairs under the canopy tent.

The rest of the mourners slip-and-slide on a muddy path up the hill. The chairs and all standing room under the tent are quickly taken. The overflow hunches miserably in the rain, their heads bowed, probably praying for this to end quickly.

A preacher steps in front of the casket and plants his feet wide as if he's going to be there a while. But he barely gets out "Dearly Beloved ... " when the widow begins to wail. The louder he talks, the louder she howls. She slips to her knees reaching toward the casket. The attendants grab her arms holding her back. After persuading her back into the chair, one attendant motions with a head nod for the preacher to wrap it up.

As her shoulders heave, the attendant and driver sit patiently at her sides. The mourners begin to trickle back to the parking lot. The attendant leans in to whisper and she stands while holding onto his arm. The rain had stopped finally, so she let the raincoat slip off her shoulders into waiting hands.

As she walks back to the limo, Wallace gawks open mouthed. Not till then, did he recognize her. He'd know that ass anywhere. He could pick it out of a lineup. Wallace drops to his knees, grabs his rain hat from his head, and wads it in his hands. His whole body tingles.

One of the Barnes crew left behind to finish the burial walks his way. "You okay, buddy?"

Wallace struggles back to his feet. "Leave me the fuck alone." He lurches haltingly down the hill toward the bus stop at the cemetery entrance.

Chapter 7

The keyboard seems to invite doom, like a loaded gun that might misfire if he touches a wrong key. Wallace types a sentence and then hits the delete key. He pecks out another sentence; reads it aloud—erases. His hands feel sticky and he wipes them on his dingy undershirt. Lacing his hands behind his head, he uncoils from his stoop and stretches back in the chair.

Dilemma wrinkles his brow. It was not unusual for him to commandeer real people as characters to manipulate like puppets on his stage. In his world, he could torture them at will. The greater their suffering, the better his story. By this point, he should be feeling the euphoria of omnipotence. But this was different. Had his fantasy become real; was he creating reality as he wrote? Had he somehow gotten sucked into his own story?

Sooner or later he'd have to shake this dread, buckle down and write. Writing was his livelihood. And it would have to be this story; the first installment was already sold. The hopelessness of a trapped animal constricts his breathing. His stomach feels like a rock.

Maybe not! A solution brightens his eyes. He could let "A Lovely Murder" stand-alone and send some other story for the next deadline. He could go out on the street right now and Shanghai a new set of characters—whip out a story so juicy Josh would forget about the serial.

His self-assured sneer fades. But what if it happens again? What if the new characters screw with his head and start writing their own story. He gets up and scowls out his second-story window into the crown of the elm that blocks his view of the street.

A grin flashes on his face. *Invent characters from scratch!* They'd be harmless, wouldn't they? Just as quickly, the smile dims back to despair. Maybe some writers created characters from their imagination, but he knew he couldn't. He'd tried that, back when he first started writing. His characters turned into jackalopes nobody believed or cardboard stiffs straight out of central casting. He'd never sold anything that way.

The pacing begins again—five steps one way to the wall, about face, five steps back. His right earlobe is red from being pulled. Or could he just steal somebody else's characters? *That's it!* He looks at the bookshelf behind the TV, at the worn spines of his secondhand book collection. There's nothing wrong with borrowing a character as long as you change the name. *Poe!* Nobody could make you sweat like his hero Poe. *Or Stevenson.* Who could forget Long John Silver?

He rushes back to the computer but sits inert staring at his reflection in the black screen. *I bet Long John Silver was real.* He imagines Stevenson sitting in a corner booth in a pub when this one-legged guy comes in with a crutch. Stevenson's Muse worked out a story to fit the character. *Same as me!* They all did it.

He feels dirty to have even considered stealing characters. *Disgusting.* For his Muse, writing a story with used character would be like having sex with a corpse. She'd cut him off forever. His Muse is so finicky, temperamental; he had long before decided it was female.

Maybe the Muse could come up with characters too? Their partnership had never worked that way. Characters had always been his job. She'd always held up her end of the bargain and came up with the story.

There was no predicting where her stories would go. Sometimes the plots turned so kinky even Josh would send them back to be toned down. *You're stifling my creativity*, he'd emailed Josh. *No tinkering with a story once it's written. You'll offend the Muse.* Josh is too plebeian to understand, but Wallace knows it's true. He never revises a story.

He sits erect, eyes closed, muscles relaxed, and tries to become a blank canvas awaiting inspiration. *She must have room to work.* In the dark cavern of his mind, a storyline materializes, but with the same old characters. *Fuck it!* He scoots his chair forward and starts writing.

Chapter 8

A Lovely Murder - Episode 2

The white envelope with DENISE *printed in block letters across the front had no address and no stamp. A neighbor must have dropped it off. Denise shuffled it with the rest of the sympathy cards and put them on the console of the Mercedes before driving on to the house.*

After dropping the bundle in the trash compactor, she halted with her finger above the start button. She dug the envelopes back out and stacked them on the island in the center of the kitchen.

"Nina!"

"Mánde?" The maid looked over her shoulder as she stirred pasta on the stove.

"Come here this second. And cut the Mexican crap. I know you speak English."

Nina wiped her hands on the apron of her starched maid outfit then swatted at the wrinkles with the back of her hand as she walked over.

"Can you write in English?"

Nina gave her a questioning look.

Denise flipped over an envelope from the top of the stack, pulled a pen from the catchall drawer, and thrust it into her hand. "Write: 'You are so wonderful to think of me in my time of grief.'"

Nina wrote it in a neat hand and looked up.

Denise signed her name at the bottom. "Now try that." Denise looked over Nina's shoulder. It looked good.

"Now." Denise twisted Nina around so she

could look directly into her eyes. "From now on, pick up the mail when it arrives each morning. Pick out the sympathy cards and answer them just like this. Put the rest of the mail on the dining room table." Nina nodded she understood and was turning back to the stove when Denise caught her arm. "Oh and answer the phone. Tell them I'm not taking calls." Denise considered how this sounded. "No, say I'm too distraught to come to the phone. Take a message if they insist. Don't bother me with any of it."

This is the response the extortionist got to his note, and later to his calls. For two days Nina took down meaningless messages and then threw them away. It wasn't until three days after the funeral, that Nina got an irate phone call and decided to leave the transcribed message on the dining room table.

I KNOW WHAT YOU DID. YOU'LL GET A CALL AT EXACTLY NOON TODAY. ANSWER IT PERSONALLY. LAST CHANCE ~~BITCH~~.

Nina had tried to obliterate the last word with her pen, but Denise could still make it out. She threw the note on top of the tuna salad Nina had laid out for her and pushed the plate away. Her whole body shook from a sudden chill.

She checked her watch—a little before noon. She went into the hall and looked down at the phone. She picked up and dialed Stanley; then slammed down the receiver before it started ringing. Stanley had warned her about calling. It was when she reached back to call him anyway that the phone started ringing. The handset clattered to the floor.

"Hello? Hello?" came a tiny squawking voice.

She fell to her knees and pulled the cord until she could reach the handset. She cautiously held it to her face. "Hel ... hello."

"Denise?" There was a pause and the voice started over. "Is this Denise Ballard?"

Although the voice was male, it sounded mechanical, like the voice of a toy robot. It occurred to her to pretend it was a wrong number or just hang up.

"Yes," she finally said.

"You killed your husband, Ms. Ballard. I know this. So don't bother denying it. I know it and I have proof. Do you understand?" The voice paused and then continued. "Do you want me to send what I have to the police?"

"I didn't do anything."

"Then you've got nothing to worry about, do you? I'm sure the police will understand about your lover buying that hammer, don't you think?"

The handset rattled to the floor again. Her hands flew out with palms outstretched as if it was a snake coiled to strike.

The miniature voice was cajoling at first and then hissed with threat. "Answer me, bitch!"

She jerked the handset off the floor, "What do you want?"

"Don't go stupid on me. I don't give a damn who murdered who—you get my drift? It's just business, see. I've got something you want, and you're gonna pay me for it. Understand?"

She looked at the handset as if the voice could be

better comprehended if she could see it. "Answer me!" it yelled.

"Yes," she heard herself say.

"Now listen up. This is what we're gonna do. "Put $500 in an envelope. Can you get your hands on $500, right now, today?"

"I'd have to go to the bank. I think I could get it at an ATM."

"That's it then. Put the money in an envelope. Go to Evergreen Park. Know where that is? Been there?"

"Yes."

"There are three park benches in a row by the east entrance. Leave the envelope on the middle bench at three PM. Then scram. Got it?"

Denise's lips twitched, formed words—said nothing.

"You got that bitch?" the robot voice yelled. "You hard of hearing or what? Say it back to me."

"Evergreen Park, middle park bench, three o'clock."

"And don't be getting wise on me. Understand? Do it all the way I say and you'll be all right." There was a click followed by a dial tone.

Chapter 9

Wallace re-reads. There's no sex or violence. He imagines Josh's disgruntled email. He composes the reply in his mind. *This sets the hook deeper in the reader. I'm building tension for the dramatic ending. The readers will know it's coming in the next episode and be waiting at the newsstand for the next issue.* He could talk shit-for-brains into anything.

He rises and starts pacing again, five steps and then five back, thinking about Denise. *Lucille Ballard?* His mind picks through his fading memory of the funeral, trying to bring the images into focus. With all the girdles or padding women wear these days, it would be impossible to positively ID a woman by her ass. But still, it could be.

If it were true, Lucille's a murderer, her and that sleazy boyfriend. That kind of broad could lure any man to murder and he's the lowlife type that would do it. Wallace realizes he'd be the only one that knows about it. The cops would never catch on.

What if he wrote her a note; gave her a call? What would be the downside? If she were innocent, she'd figure he was just another crackpot. She'd expect that, with all the publicity, her being high profile and all. She'd just forget it and that would be the end. But if she were guilty, she'd pay anything to keep it quiet. Wallace thinks of the newscast with the stone archway in the background. *How much is she worth?*

Wallace stops by Burger King for his usual Whopper before walking on to the library. He goes straight to the computer terminals and logs into the email account he'd created there. This is where he orders his porn and keeps track of his homies that might be wanted by the cops.

He first Googles Randolph Ballard and finds a long list of newspaper articles about civic awards. There is a wedding announcement published in the *Morning Gazette* last November. Lucille's maiden name was Sweeny. Another article just a month ago is about them buying stuff at a Rotary Club silent auction. No pictures with either article, however.

When he enters Lucille Sweeny into Facebook, he hits the jackpot. There is nothing from the last few days, but she is definitely an active user. There's a history of chitchat with girlfriend Myra. Myra's last post:

> **Unless he's got a magical twelve-inch dick that holds the krabby patty secret ingredient, he's replaceable. Stop putting up with his shit.**

He browses through their banter going back two years until he comes to a photo Myra had posted of a nude passed out face down on a poolside picnic table cluttered with liquor and beer bottles. Disheveled blonde hair covers her face, but the ass looks like Lucille's. Lucille replied back:

> **Email me at bestbj69@yahoo. I've got pics too, Honeypot. Want to see 'em on your page?**

Wallace switches to Yahoo and types in the address. He puts "Sorry about Randolph" in the subject line and hits ENTER. There is no error message, so it must still be a valid address. He starts a new message with the subject "Emergency!"

> **I know about you and the guy with the slicked-back hair. I know what you did to your husband. Email me back tomorrow at twelve noon or the rest of the world will know also.**

He stares at the screen, going over in his mind the possible ramifications. *What the hell.* He hits ENTER.

Chapter 10

The next day at twelve-thirty, Wallace logs into his email at the library. He is surprised to see two responses:

Go fuck yourself.

Then time marked fifteen minutes later:

What do you want?

Wallace's face stretches to a grin. *Bingo!*

Money.

You got nothing on me.

Look on your Facebook page in ten minutes if you don't think so.

You're going to jail for blackmail.

Maybe. You want to call the cops, or should I? How about we stop the happy horseshit. Are you in or not? You've got five minutes left.

Wallace pulls at his right earlobe and watches the screen for three minutes before the reply:

How much?

"Yes!" Wallace yells out before he can catch himself. When he looks up, the librarian at the checkout counter is scowling at him like he'd farted in church. Wallace humps his shoulders and gives her a *not me* expression. He points discretely at the nerd at the computer terminal on the opposite side of the table. After the librarian resumes what she was doing, he types:

I will email you again in thirty minutes. Be there!!!!

He waits two more minutes before he clicks ENTER. Let her sweat this time.

Wallace switches to Google Maps and goes to street view. He finds a farm road outside of town and simulates driving down it until he comes to a clapboard farmhouse with a long dirt driveway. On the near side of the driveway is a rusty mailbox and beside it a yellow tube for the *Morning Gazette*. After zooming in to read the number on the mailbox, he goes back to email and starts typing.

Tomorrow at seven PM, deliver an envelope containing

If he demands too much, she might balk. No need to be greedy. He could always go back later for more.

$1000 to 505 Buckner Road in Franklin County. Put it in the yellow newspaper tube next to the mailbox. Turn around in the driveway and go straight home. I'll be watching.

He waits until the thirty minutes is up and clicks ENTER. She replies immediately:

How do I know you won't post something anyway?

As long as I get what I want, I've got no reason. I don't care if some chick and her boyfriend off the husband. He probably needed killing anyway. It's no skin off my nose either way.

What's to keep you from coming back later and wanting more?

Chat's over. Tomorrow. Seven sharp. No funny business.

He deletes all the messages, including the sent and trash files, before shutting down.

Chapter 11

At dusk the following day, Wallace's cab passes the farmhouse. He twists to look at the empty road behind him through the rear window. The cab turns around at the entrance to a pasture and drives back.

"That's my house up yonder on the right. Pull over to that mailbox. Wife left me divorce papers to sign in that newspaper tube beside it."

Wallace rolls down the rear door window as the cab coasts to a stop, stretching his arm through the window to grab a thick manila envelope.

"You suppose to sign it and put it back?"

"Yeah, that's what she wants. But I gotta read it first. She's probably asking for the gold fillings outta my teeth, you know what I mean?"

"Where to now, buddy," the Pakistani asks over his shoulder with his heavy accent.

Wallace cringes at the eyes with a red dot between them looking back at him in the rearview mirror. "I ain't your buddy, buddy. Go back to where we started. I'll bring this back later."

Wallace puts the envelope to his nose and sniffs to see if he can smell the money. He imagines he can.

"I want you to pick me up in front of the dry cleaners at eight. I'm going downtown—someplace expensive." Wallace sits back and imagines himself in a limo. "You know any women? I only want the good stuff; high dollar white women, get me? I've got some celebrating to do."

Chapter 12

Wallace delays the joy of opening the envelope until he's sitting at his desk. He thumbs through the stack of crisp twenties before taking out half of the bills and arranging them face-front in his wallet. When he returns the wallet in his back pocket, he squirms around in the seat enjoying the feel of the added bulk. "Damn!" he shouts jumping up. The rest of the money in the envelope he deposits between March and April in his *Hustler* collection on the shelf behind the TV.

This was manna from heaven that just fell in his lap. Not that he didn't deserve a lucky break, but it almost seemed too easy. He paces with a scowl tugging at his ear, thinking back through what he'd done, trying to think of ways he might get caught. *Home free*, he concludes with a puff of relief.

This money was pocket change for Lucille. But it might put her in a bind if he asked for more right away. He'd have to wait until the estate is settled, until she can get to the Ballard fortune without suspicion. *Have to play it smart*. He'd lay off for now, but this was like money in the bank.

Wallace returns to the desk chair and closes his eyes, trying to clear his mind to finish episode two of "A Lovely Murder," but the beautiful green faces of Andrew Jackson are still smiling at him. No worry about the rent for a while. He didn't need Josh anymore. He grinned with the thought of his email: *Kiss my ass, you fag!*

Maybe he could write something serious for a change—finish that memoir he'd started about his stepdad beating him all the time, let people know why he burned down the house. They're all dead now, nobody left to dispute his version of things.

"Hot damn, I'll do it!" he says aloud with maniacal glee. He'd kill them again; make 'em suffer even worse this time.

Then his face turns to gloom when his thoughts return to Josh. If he reneged on the "Lovely Murder" serial, Josh would probably put him on a blacklist with other publishers. *The asshole.* He slumps sullenly looking back at his reflection in the black computer screen until suddenly he jerks erect and sticks out his chin. *Integrity.* He'd promised four episodes; so he was damn well gonna deliver. He was a man of his word; everybody knew that.

Chapter 13

(LM E2 continued)

Denise turned off Fuller into the parking lot and found an empty space between two other cars as far away from the park entrance as she could. When she leaned forward, she could look past the other cars and see the row of green benches beside the stone arched entranceway.

A little boy ran out of the archway, then a mother emerged scowling and scolding. The boy sheepishly walked back and took her hand. She walked him to a van, buckled him in, and drove away.

Denise watched the entrance a minute longer before pulling down her floppy hat and brisk-walking to the park bench and back. She scrunched down in the plush Mercedes seat and stared through the door windows of the car next to her at the distorted patch of white against the background of green.

A black teen came through the arches hand-in-hand with a blonde girl. They were giggling to each other and neither looked at the bench. An hour later, an old man approached on the sidewalk led by a terrier on a leash. He glanced at the envelope, hesitated; then the dog pulled him through the entrance into the park.

The sun was setting in front of her and she squinted against the glare. The car was getting stuffy and she thought about starting the engine and running the air conditioner, then decided against it.

She leaned her head against the seatback, determined to wait it out.

She startled from a doze, awakened by a horrible dream of a robot chasing her. Her heart raced as she tried to remember why she was there. The cars that had been beside hers were gone now. When the streetlight above the entrance flickered on, she could make out the glare of white on the bench and felt relieved.

A stooped figure shuffled into the light thrown by the streetlight like a character entering from offstage. He pushed a grocery cart heaped with plastic bags between the boxwoods beside the entrance. After strolling to the park benches, he looked down at the envelope then around him in all directions. As he sat, the envelope disappeared. An apple was in his hand when it came out of his pocket.

Lucille watched him gnaw at the apple slowly with toothless gums. It seemed like forever before he pitched the core over his shoulder into the flowerbed. Again, his head pivoted surveying for anyone watching before bringing out the envelope. His tongue leaked between his lips as he folded back the flap and squinted inside. He stuck a finger in the envelope to explore for something he might not have seen and then flipped it onto the sidewalk.

He pulled a toboggan from his grimy black overcoat and tugged it onto his head. Slowly, methodically, he removed the overcoat and covered himself as he reclined on the bench. He drew the toboggan down over his eyes and turned on his side to face the back of the bench.

Lucille waited. The man fidgeted, adjusting his hips to the slots in the bench, and then lay perfectly *still. After checking that no one else was around, she quietly opened her car door. As she strolled by the bench, she bent and picked up the envelope. It wasn't until she reached the end of the block that she looked inside. The money was gone. A note was scrawled onto the inside of the envelope flap.*

STUPID BITCH. THE COPS WILL BE WAITING WHEN YOU RETURN HOME UNLESS YOU DO EXACTLY AS I SAY. WAVE IF YOU AGREE.

She turned and looked back at the park bench. The street bum hadn't moved. She searched the sidewalk in both directions. There was nobody. She tentatively lifted her arm and waved anyway.

End – episode 2

Chapter 14

"Get out! Get out! I've got to work. El scramo!" Wallace doesn't know the words in Mexican, or Hindu, or whatever.

She dresses slowly and then goes to the bathroom to tidy her makeup. After coming out, she stands by the door with one hand on her hip and her other palm up. Wallace places twenties in her hand one at a time, pausing after each one, hoping the hand will close.

He slams the door and teeters trying to align himself to the swaying room. He lurches to the sofa and throws himself onto his back. When he closed his eyes, the room begins to tumble so he anchors one foot on the floor. He stares at the overhead light fixture counting the bug carcasses silhouetted inside the frosted globe while waiting for nausea to subside. Losing track of the count, he starts over several times before falling asleep.

Sunset is already dimming the room when Wallace awakes. Thirst drives him staggering toward the bathroom. His shoulder glances off the doorframe. After splashing water on his face, he slurps from his cupped hands.

Looking at himself in the vanity mirror, he takes stock. Considering the steaks at the Ritz, the tour of the downtown bars afterward, and the bottle of twenty-year-old Scotch he'd brought home, it had been an expensive evening. For a short little shit, she drank like a fish. At the end, he'd guzzled the last of the Scotch to keep her from wasting it all.

Wallace plops down in his writing chair. A smile emerges on his face. All told, last night had been a success. In the breakthrough novel he was going to write, his hero would hang out in swanky bars with notorious gangsters and slinky broads. Last night could be chalked up to research. *Can't write about what you don't know.*

The icons of American literature, after all, were drunks and whoremongers before they became famous writing about it. Like him, they were exceptional liars. He could do all that. He felt part of a brotherhood. Already last night's prostitute grew taller and more voluptuous in his memory. She would have fallen madly in love if he'd let her stay.

Chapter 15

Wallace grabs the wad of newspaper off the counter before sitting at his corner table. "Hey Vera, what day is it?"

"Hell, I don't know, Wally. Look on the paper."

It's Friday, the day Stanley planned to meet Denise. Before Vera brings the coffee, he moves ahead to the next table.

Sure enough, Denise—*eh, Lucille*—comes in at ten. He pops the paper open in front of his face as she walks by. Over the paper he can see the swinging glass door open again; below the paper, bare ankles in oxford loafers walk by. *It's him all right.* Wallace flinches when the guy bumps the back of his chair.

Lucille's urgent whisper chirps like a nest of newly hatched birds. Wallace catches a few words, "email … extortion," blurted out as she fights against hysteria. "What am I going to do … ?" Her voice trails off into a low whine.

Stanley can be heard perfectly. "Put a plug in it. Get a grip. Meet me down the street in a few minutes and we'll talk this through."

Under Wallace's paper, the sockless loafers hesitate beside him before turning toward the door.

"Just coffee," Lucille says when Vera comes over with her order pad.

Vera's feet turn to leave and then turn back. "You OK, Sweetie?"

"Men. You just can't trust 'em."

"Know what you mean, Sweetie." Vera scurries away and returns with the coffee. "Seems every woman's gotta learn that lesson for herself—the hard way," she says before returning behind the counter.

Wallace hears Lucille fumbling in her purse for money, or maybe a handkerchief. There's a sob, then a sniffle before she gets up in a rush for the door. Wallace is getting up to follow when Vera slides a plate of bacon and eggs onto his table.

"I didn't order no breakfast."

"But—"

"I didn't order nothing," he scoffs as he hurries past her to the door.

Lucille pulls down a floppy hat and walks with head slumped for a block and half to the Dixie Hotel. Wallace is familiar with the Dixie. In a bygone era, it had been a popular destination. Back in 1955, Hopalong Cassidy had stayed there while performing at the county fair. An autographed picture of him with his horse hangs behind the bar. This section of the city gradually became seedy, and by the eighties, the hotel had gone bankrupt. The rooms were converted to efficiency apartments that rented by the week. Wallace himself had stayed there a few times after being evicted from one apartment or another—*while looking for something more suitable.*

The bar in the back of the lobby is really just a pickup station for the whores who have rooms upstairs. It wouldn't be open until after dark. When Wallace walks by the plate glass window, Lucille's legs are ascending the scarred wood stairway beside the lobby, that lovely booty swaying with each step.

Wallace shops in a second-hand store on the far side of the street, staying close to the display window to watch the Dixie Hotel entrance. An hour later, Lucille comes to the lobby window and makes a cell phone call, then stands back from the window until a yellow cab stops in front. She scurries out and scrunches down in the back seat before the cab pulls back into traffic.

Wallace loiters behind the store window waiting for the guy— Stanley, or whatever—to come out. He must live there.

Chapter 16

A LOVELY MURDER – Episode 3

At the café on Friday, Denise's voice modulated between spitting anger and whining desperation. When Stanley held out his palms for her to stop, she bit her lip, face contorted as if her rant might explode.

Stanley mouthed the words "Not here," as he put money on the table beside his coffee. He leaned across the table as if to give her a peck on the cheek. "See you in fifteen minutes," he whispered. He stood and surveyed the other customers as he stretched. Nobody looked his way except the cook behind the counter. He pointed to the money on the table and walked casually out the door, turning in the direction of the Dixie.

When Denise walked into the hotel room, their little love nest, she felt safe again. Stanley closed and locked the door behind her and turned with that unnerving stare. She never knew what it meant. Her frantic explanations began again. It wasn't her fault; she'd done everything the way he'd told her.

"Shut up and come here."

When she froze, unable to make her legs obey, Stanley reached out with both hands to her throat and pulled her close in front of his icy blue eyes. Her eyes clenched shut waiting for the hands to tighten. His lips touched hers lightly and then moved to her cheeks, sucking up the tears that had squeezed out.

"But what——?" His finger pressed to her lips

stopped her.

He undressed her slowly, relishing each button that came free and the sound of the zipper lowering inch by inch. Her anxiety slipped away with each layer of clothing, her tense body melted under his spell. Reaching past her to the nightstand, he tuned the radio to a hard-rock station and turned up the volume. "I'm gonna make you scream."

After removing his shirt, he paused to graze over her body; light kisses to her forehead, the tip of her nose, and both sides of her neck. The tip of his tongue massaged her nipples, then the chill as he blew lightly until they became stiff. He turned her to face away and began again. Lips trailed down her spine leaving goosebumps. Hot breath on her legs made her quiver as if being brushed with a feather.

Her husband had given her everything money could buy. But he couldn't make her too weak to stand, unleash a thousand butterflies to flutter beneath her skin. Whereas her husband had the musty smell of old money, Stanley smelled of sweat and cheap whiskey. It swallowed her whole. She was his instrument to be played, his possession to be consumed. Before Stanley, if a girlfriend had tried to explain this ecstasy, she would have laughed out loud.

Afterward, he rolled onto his back, his arms thrown back on the pillow behind his head, away from his sweaty body. His eyes fluttered then closed as if slipping into sleep. She swung her leg across his, nuzzling her cheek against his hairy chest.

"Too hot," he said pushing her away. "The AC in this place is on the fritz again."

She waited quietly as Stanley stared at the ceiling.

He twisted to turn down the radio before propping on an elbow to look at her. "Somebody saw us, noticed us together. When your picture ran in the paper, he remembered and put two and two together" Stanley's finger pushed a curl out of her face. "Nobody's fault, just a bad break."

She smiled in relief and took a full breath.

"He'll contact you again, want more money. Just play along, for now; give him whatever he wants. Act dumb and scared. Whatever you do, don't hang around and try to spot him yourself next time. He's too smart for that. Just let me know where and when the drop is and I'll take it from there. He can't hide forever. He'll slip up. He'll be toast when that happens."

"I can't do it," His face wrinkled in her bleared vision.

"Yes, you can, Babe. And you will. We're in this together, all the way to our eyeballs. We gotta do what we gotta do from here on in."

Her face stiffened as she tried to understand.

"Say it."

"Gotta do what we gotta do."

"I'll take care of this Bozo. Don't worry about it."

Chapter 17

After deleting the junk mail, there was only a single message from Josh:

> **Wallace Rose,**
>
> **We can't accept a serial sight unseen, Buck-O. We'll have to hold your check on the first episode until we receive the story in total. It'll have to be approved by the editorial staff. That's *Suspense* policy.**
>
> **Looking forward to reading the next exciting episodes. Send them ASAP.**
>
>

Josh Billings,
Executive Editor
>

Executive Editor? Who does shit-for-brains think he's talking to? Unless he's gotten a dog from the pound recently, there is no "we" in Suspense Publishing. Wallace is in contact with the other contributors to *Suspense.* A fellow writer who lives close to Josh occasionally helps with the magazine distribution.

Suspense is printed on the sly off a press in Josh's hometown that normally publishes the monthly Realtors Association magazine. Josh has a sweetheart deal with the press operator assigned to do maintenance on Sundays. He leaves his van loaded with paper stock parked at the loading dock before daylight every third Sunday. A memory stick and three one hundred-dollar bills are in the glove box. After sunset, he drives away with the next edition of *Suspense.* The press operator would swear on a stack of Bibles, he isn't part of Suspense Publishing. Josh gets his jollies pretending to be some big-time operation. *The dickhead.*

Josh,

My lawyer is reviewing our emails now, but I believe we already have a contract for the short story "*A Lovely Murder.*" *Suspense* is obligated to pay before publication according to the previously agreed terms.

I just received Episode 2 from my editor. After I check it over, I'll forward it on to you. The remaining episodes will follow on Monday.

Since this is a serial, I will expect full payment for all 25,373 words before the first episode is printed. This is the standard agreement in our industry.

Respectfully,
Wallace Rose

Wallace switches to Google and looks for the Realty Association in Spotsboro, Illinois. An anonymous email will blow Suspense Publishing up like a cheap pipe bomb. He starts composing the email and then sits back. Better to wait to see if he gets a check first; wait until it clears the bank. He should send this email from the library anyway.

He goes to the bookcase for another withdrawal. Two hundred bucks. He counts it twice. That's all that's left.

Chapter 18

(LM E3 continued)

Denise stood at the picture window, like she did every day at two, staring down the long winding driveway, waiting for the stubby white van to stop at her mailbox. If there were a blackmail note, it would have been delivered last night. It was out there now. But Nina would give her one of those "el stupido" looks if asked to pick up the mail before it ran.

After Nina retrieved the mail, Denise paced in front of the dining room, glancing in at the white stack of envelopes in the center of the walnut table each time she passed the doorway. When she screwed up enough courage, she dashed in and stirred through the envelopes. Bills—nothing but bills. There was a moment of relief and then despondency set in again.

She was tired of being cooped up like this with no one to talk to. She longed to resume her Tuesday lunches at Armand's with the girls—get tipsy, gossip, giggle. But Stanley was right; it wouldn't look right. And after a few glasses of merlot, she might let something slip and make things even more complicated.

Stanley had insisted they not see each other, or even exchange phone calls for a month. It had floored her that he could just give her up so easily. "Need to let the trail go cold. Gotta do what we gotta do." It had felt like a warning. "In a month, start hanging out nights at Armand's with your girlfriends. I'll come over and ask you to dance. We'll act like we've never met before. Got it? Tell the girls you've made a date. We'll go from there."

The month was up this Friday. She sighed with relief that her period of mourning, her celibacy, would soon be over. She'd already set up the night out with the girls. "I've just got to get out of this house, away from the memory of what happened," she'd pleaded on the phone between sniffles.

She walked into the den and crumpled into the overstuffed chair by the phone table. Nina scurried around with her dust mop, banging pots in the kitchen to make her jump. It was just too much. "Get out!" she yelled before catching herself. When Nina's head poked around a corner, "Take the rest of the day off, Honey. See you tomorrow."

After the front door closed, her ears rang with the quiet of the cavernous room. As the sun lowered, sinuous shadows of trees through the sheer curtains elongated across the hardwood floor like grasping arms.

She grabbed a remote and instantly orange flames erupted in the fireplace. The orange flickers made the enormous house even more foreboding. The overhead lights would be worse, too stark, too revealing.

It seemed her whole life had been spent in this chair, nursing coffee in the mornings and wine in the afternoons, imagining every possible threat or demand that grating little voice might make.

Maybe she should just give the number on caller ID to the police. A degenerate stalker making threating phone calls to the home of a grieving widow. It would be some low-life's word against the word of the wife of a bank president, a contributor to the Police Benevolence Society.

The blackmailer probably had nothing more than, "I saw this woman that looked like her ... " The police would discount anything he'd say. But what if he had pictures, a compromising cell phone shot of her and Stanley that couldn't be explained away?

Late into the nights, she mulled her predicament through the fog of champagne. This worthless criminal would forever be a cloud of doom hanging over her. It might be months before he called again, the next demand, his threat of exposure. Stanley was right; this man had to be eliminated.

Stanley had bragged confidently that he would take care of it. He is sly and ruthless enough. She had seen him in action. But there was nothing they could do until the blackmailer made contact. Stanley would probably insist they stay apart until this threat was over. She'd go crazy if he did that.

Sometimes she wondered. What did she really know about Stanley anyway? He'd given few clues about himself and Google couldn't find any trace of him. She didn't even know where he lived, unless it was that dumpy room at the Dixie. If push came to shove, a man like Stanley could just fade away, leaving her to face the music alone.

They'd first met on the mid-town bridge over Falls River when he offered to help her throw the toy ducks she'd purchased over the bridge railing at the charity duck race. Her gloomy face softened as she remembered how his strong hands had taken control of her arms, how immediate and thorough her seduction had been.

Alcohol added glow to her memories of their first embrace, their first kiss, and the first time they had met at the Dixie. She chided herself for giving in to paranoia. They were madly in love. After all, it had been Stanley that had given her hope, suggested a way out of the drab life she'd married into. He'd killed to have her.

The phone rang. It was probably her best friend Myra, the only one who would call this late. "Hello, Squirt Blossom."

"Squirt Blossom?" It was the robot voice. Her mouth jerked wide in a silent scream. As she listened to his distorted chuckle, humiliation rose like bile in her throat. The tears squeezing out of her clenched eyes were not from fear any longer, but unbridled hate. She couldn't let him detect the rage in her voice.

"No, no! I thought it was somebody else, a friend calling me back."

"Listen up. I need more money. Something's come up and I need a thousand—"

"Stop!" She paused to gain control over a seething shriek. "I've got somebody on hold. Call me back."

"Get rid of 'em."

"Yeah, I will. Call me back in ten minutes."

"Ten minutes."

When she heard the dial tone, she slammed the handset into the cradle as if she were clubbing the blackmailer in the mouth. She picked it up and slammed it again and again. "You son-of-a-bitch!"

She bent forward into her lap and cried in gasping spasms. It had been his taunting laughter that she had not been prepared for. Like her father and all the other bullies she'd known since puberty, he'd dismissed her as a mindless joke.

If he had detected fear, he would have goaded her further, called her names—whore, stupid. The teasing would have continued until he heard her break, turn to mush, begin to beg. And then he would laugh even louder at her whining pleas for mercy.

The blackmailer had a face now—or many faces. She'd known him all her life. She wiped her eyes with the hem of her dress and clenched her jaw as she stared defiantly into the fire. With quick thinking, she'd taken back control. In these ten minutes, she would compose herself, come up with a plan. It would be her turn when the bastard called back.

The flames from the fireplace glimmered on a demonic face. The amber flickers dancing in her eyes seemed to come from smoldering within.

End – episode 3

Chapter 19

A LOVELY MURDER – Episode 4

Denise was wearing black when she walked into Armand's with a box wrapped in white sepia paper tied with a pink ribbon.

"I have your table ready, Ms. Ballard."

The Maître d' pulled out a chair at a table beside the front window. Sparkling silverware and a napkin folded like a tall drum major's hat were arranged on the white linen tablecloth. A budvase of fresh cut flowers sat in the center.

"Will there be just one tonight, Ms. Ballard?"

"I'll be meeting friends here for a birthday party later, but I'll be eating alone."

"May I speak for the entire staff in extending our sympathy for your loss of Mr. Ballard. We're so glad to see you here again."

"Thank you, James. I just couldn't stay away any longer." She reached in her purse for a handkerchief to dab her eyes. "Everybody is like family to me here."

"May I bring you a cocktail? Some wine?"

"I really shouldn't … Yes, bring me a Manhattan, to calm my nerves."

"Right away, Ms. Ballard."

The tenseness in her shoulders thawed more with every sip of her cocktail. On the sidewalk out front, young women streamed by in bright sundresses and sandals on their way to the boutiques nearby. A stern defiance took her face. She'd had enough of being cloistered in black. All that would end tonight.

She finished her drink in one swallow and held up her finger for another. Tomorrow she would call Myra for a shopping binge, dress in red. Maybe the period of mourning should be longer, but she was tired of being a widow.

The street grew darker outside as she ate. Red and blue neon reflections streaked across the shiny roof and hood of the sedan across the street, the loaner she'd been given at the dealership when she left her Mercedes for service. She'd arrived before the rush of evening diners so she could have that parking spot. From there she would have a clear view of the entrance to the alley beside Armand's.

Her heart began to race when she glanced at her watch. The blackmail pickup was in thirty minutes; barely time to review her plan one last time.

When Darth Vader voice called back last night, she'd called his bluff.

"Nobody's going to believe you. You'll be just another swindler trying to cash in on a tragedy. It will be your word against mine. Guess who's going to win?"

"I've got proof, I tell you. And even if it doesn't land you in jail, you'll never live down the suspicion. After I put out my stuff, everybody's going to treat you different."

"Maybe ... OK. One last payment and then we're through. Come back again, and I'll go to the cops. Understand? We'll both take our chances. Got it? And no more park benches in the middle of the afternoon. If someone sees me at a place like that, they'll know something's up. Call back in ten minutes and I'll let you know where I'll drop the

money." She'd hung up before he had a chance to protest. She hadn't needed the ten minutes but wanted him to think the drop location was a last-minute idea.

"Look, no funny business—" he blurted when he called back.

"Shut up! I'm going to meet a friend for dinner at Armand's tomorrow night. I'll leave it there. Know how to get there? Not one of your usual restaurants, I'm sure.

"I've been there."

"Well, there's an alley beside it with a dumpster in the back. The money will be in a box with a pink ribbon on it just inside the lid. Pick it up after seven."

"I ain't going through—"

"Then don't, Asshole. Maybe some other bum will find it before the city hauls it away. Either way, this is our last conversation." Again, she hung up before he could reply.

"Would you like another? James startled her.

"Oh, I guess I'd slipped off for a moment. Yes, I'll have another. But first, I've got to go to the ladies' room."

As James pulled out her chair, Denise slipped the cardboard coaster from under her drink into her purse and gathered the purse and box in her arms. On her way down the hallway to the restrooms, she passed the emergency exit. She'd discovered this door to the alley by mistake late one night while partying with Myra. In a stupor, she'd mistaken the door for the restroom and found herself outside. The fire escape only opened from the inside, so she'd had to walk around and come back in the front door. Myra had laughed her ass off.

Denise bent to the water fountain beside the exit twisting her head to see if anybody was looking. As the door closed behind her, she inserted the drink coaster between the door lock and door facing. The dumpster against the wall at the end of the alley was barely visible in the indirect light from the street. She walked as fast as she could in pumps. The spoiled food smell flooded out when she raised the lid. Holding her breath, she placed the box just inside the door, then picked it up again and flung it into a pile of slop further in. Let the SOB dig for it.

Her confident grin morphed back into the somber face of bereavement before she got back to her table.

"Here you are, Madam." James placed a fresh Manhattan before her and cleared away the empty glass.

Chapter 20

Wallace admires his progress on episode four of "A Lovely Murder." This is way too good for the chicken feed he'd be getting from *Suspense*. Maybe he could get out of the contract with Josh and send the story to *Harpers* or the *New Yorker*. *Playboy*! *Playboy* would jump on a story like this. Joseph Heller, Jack Kerouac, and Kurt Vonnegut, all the greats, broke into the big time with *Playboy*. This is his destiny.

Wallace switches to email.

> **Josh,**
>
> **I've just received a message from my copyright atturnies, Siegel and Lebovitz, informing me you are in breach of contract. They have prepared a lawsuit seeking $1,000,000 damages to be filed Monday. However, I have informed them that I prefer to retract my manuscript "A Lovely Murder" to avoid a legal dispute with my long-time friend and associet.**
>
> > **Regards,**
> > **Wallace Rose, Esquire**

Wallace switches back to word-processing and stares at a blank page as he thinks about the fame coming his way. *Playboy* would want to include a photograph in the interview section. Might as well send it with the manuscript. The computer times out and his scruffy face reflects on the black screen. A haircut would help. Trim the stubble so it looks intentional. Buy a pipe. Tomorrow, he'll fix himself up and take a selfie in the mirror with his cell phone.

Chapter 21

Denise got up and switched to the chair on the opposite side of the table so she could watch the sidewalk in front of the blind alley. She waited, nursing her drink, determined not to get sloshed.

A half-hour went by, and then she stiffened in her chair. He was waiting for her to leave! Of course! He was watching her through the restaurant window right now. She searched the storefronts across the street for a face turned her way. He would be hidden by the glare of one of those display windows.

She held up her finger to get James's attention.

"Whoa! I guess I'm out of practice, James. I won't be able to drive if I keep this up. Better bring me a check." She reached out and touched him on the elbow as he turned. "When my friend shows up, tell her I wasn't feeling well, will you? Oh, and will you call me a cab? No sense getting another ticket."

"Sure thing, Ms. Ballard."

She walked across the street and waited in front of her loaner car parked parallel to the curb. When the cab arrived, she yelled her home address through the closed front window. The driver nodded that he understood, but she yelled it again as if he hadn't.

At the corner, she tapped on the back of the cabbie's headrest. "Take me around the block and bring me back to that same spot."

The cabbie gave her a "what-the-hell" look in the mirror.

"Back to the same place, understand? Here ..."

She scrounged in her purse. "Here's a twenty." His expression changed to "whatever-you-say."

When the cab stopped, she eased out the cab door and into the passenger seat of her car. After adjusting the rearview mirror to look behind, she pulled on a floppy hat from her purse and scrunched low in the seat.

Twenty minutes later, a tall man in a loose-fitting hoody approached from behind. She held her breath as he walked by, certain that the door would fly open. Instead, he crossed in front of her car without looking in and jogged across the street to Armand's. He strolled past the alley and stopped to look in the department store window next door. Five minutes later, he reversed directions and vanished into the dark alley.

By the flash of a match, she could make out the outline of his hooded head as he leaned against the side of the alley. The tiny orange glow of a cigarette floated in the darkness, blooming brightly when he took a drag.

She needed to see his face, be able to describe him to Stanley. If he made the pickup without her getting a good look, he would escape her trap. He would have outsmarted her again. He'd be emboldened to call again, call her names, humiliate her. The overload of adrenaline that fear had pumped into her system when he'd passed her car fueled anger now.

The orange dot twisted through the blackness to the far wall of the alley and bounced to the asphalt. He would be walking back to the dumpster to get her money. He wouldn't get away with this!

She scooted to the driver's seat and started the motor. When the headlights came on automatically, she switched them off. The street was empty. She idled across the street and nosed into the alley as if turning around. When she turned on the headlights, he was bent into the dumpster with his back to her. Her tires squealed against the asphalt. He turned to face the headlights just before her bumper pinned him to the dumpster.

The horn beeped when the impact threw her chest against the steering wheel, but she continued to press the accelerator while gasping for breath. He wasn't getting away; she was in control now. The tires began to squeal again before she lifted her foot. His body was flopped onto the hood, pivoted at his broken, if not severed, legs.

She shifted to reverse and slowly backed away. He slid off the car hood, out of sight at first, until she backed far enough away to see his torso crumpled face-forward onto his legs.

With his hands, he pushed himself into a seated position leaning back against the dumpster. His head, face still hidden by the hood, tilted forward over the pant legs oozing red into a growing pool. His head slowly rose. One hand stretched out in front to shield his eyes from the one surviving headlight as he squinted through the windshield.

His head fell forward again, shoulders jerking in spasms. While holding himself propped back against the dumpster with one arm, he pulled back the sweatshirt hood with the other hand. He pointed at her with his middle finger and laughed riotously. She could hear his scornful hoots through the windshield.

"You stupid bitch," he yelled.

She shifted back into drive and floored it. The bumper caught Stanley at eye level and drove him *back into the dumpster. His head popped open like a dropped melon.*

End — final episode

Chapter 22

"WALLACE ROSE – The Untold Story" he types at the top of the screen and then sits perfectly still staring at the title. Only his eyes twitch when an idea passes through his brain. Finally, he pounds the desktop with the flat of his hands and goes to the fridge for a drink. He pops the tab of a twelve-ounce can of Clamato and takes a swallow before refilling it with the last of a bottle of vodka he also keeps in the refrigerator. His face draws into disgust with his next swallow. The taste is terrible, but sometimes it's required to get the old creative juices flowing.

When he comes back to his desk, he stands behind his chair and turns his face to the ceiling. "I'm here. Let the record show that I've been waiting patiently all morning for my Muse to show up. Stupid bitch!"

Wallace bites his upper lip, horrified at what he'd just said. His eyes move around the room, looking into the dark corners. He forces a giggle. "Just joking," he says, but he suspects it's too late to retract the blasphemy.

The computer dings indicating an incoming email. Probably Josh, he's always online. The pervert's got nothing better to do than pump his meat.

> **Wallace,**
> **Wowee! I'm scared to death. According to Google, Siegel and Lebovitz is an importer located in San Francisco specializing in blow-up dolls made in China. You can't even spell attorney without spell-check. I'm tired of putting up with your bullshit. I'd pull your whole story if the first installment weren't already at the printer.**

The Muse of Wallace Rose

I did a quick read of the remaining installments you just sent. The story's OK, but I found enough grammatical and spelling errors that I'll have to get one of my copy editors to clean it up. Do you even have an editor? If so, you need to fire him/her/it. I'll have to charge you back two cents per word for the editing cost.

And who is Lucille? You changed the name of the dame in the story from Denise to Lucille in episode 2, for Christ sake! Where's your head?

Let me summarize our deal in case you get confused again. You offered me four installments of "A Lovely Murder" under the same arrangements as our previous transactions. You sent me the copy and I accepted. I made payment in full (minus the editing) to your PayPal account. The installments will be printed in sequential issues of *Suspense*. Explain this to Siegel and Lebovitz. Maybe they'll give you a discount on a doll.

Josh Billings,
Executive Editor

Wallace checks his PayPal account. The payment transaction from Suspense Publishing is complete. Josh indeed has undisputed rights to "A Lovely Murder." *Damn!* The jerk-off had him—unless. If Suspense Publishing went out of business before the next publication date, then there really would be a breach of contract. The story would revert to him and he could sell it again. *Paid twice for the same story!* Wallace jumps up in a huff. He shucks the pajama bottoms and struggles into jeans he found crumpled in the corner. By this time tomorrow, Suspense Publishing will be history. No bottom-feeding publisher is going to outsmart him.

Chapter 23

After Wallace hits ENTER on the library computer firing off his anonymous message to the Spotsboro Realty Association, with copies to the Spotsboro Chamber of Commerce and the Spotsboro Daily News, he feels in control again.

He switches to the search engine and finds the local Crime Stopper Hotline site. Might as well give Lucille what she deserves while he's at it. It would be safer to make the call from a phone booth, so he jots the phone number on a sticky-note for later.

But why kill the golden goose? He should give Lucille one more chance. If she refuses to pay, she will deserve having a dime dropped on her. Wallace logs out and wanders through the aisles of books as he formulates a foolproof plan. After an hour, he logs back on.

> **Lucille,**
>
> **Thank you for your contribution to our cause. In consideration of your generosity, I would like to send you the flattering pictures of you and your companion. You seem like such a loving couple. Please reply immediately with your mailing address. Wouldn't want these pictures to wind up in the wrong mailbox.**
>
> **Your friend,**
> **Longdong Silver**

As he'd hoped, Lucille was at her computer.

> **You know my address. What do you want?**

Lucille,

Yes, I do. Thanks for reminding me. However, I don't have your cell phone number. I may need to talk with you about the details of our transaction.

Longdong

The response was not immediate this time.

Limpdick,

As you know, my friend can be violent when he gets angry. You're playing a dangerous game.

Lucy, Lucy, Lucy,

Oh, I'm so sorry if I've made you angry. Not to worry. After this contribution, you'll receive a package in your mailbox, and you won't hear from me again—ever.

Take a cab from your home to the previous deposit location. Leave $2000 at precisely 2 PM tomorrow. I'll be watching and if you do anything other than what I instruct, I'll address my envelope of pictures to the Morning Gazette.

Reply with your cell phone number. I won't ask again.

Longerdong (you excite me)

Wallace waits; concerned he's overplayed his hand. Desperation subsides when the message containing her phone number pops up. He logs off and goes to the public phone in the foyer of the library to verify the number.

"Hello."

Wallace recognizes Lucille's yappy-dog voice from the café and hangs up. *Game on.*

Chapter 24

The next morning Wallace leisurely strolls the three blocks to Walmart. He inspects all the cell phones on display at the electronics counter and uses the last of Lucille's money to purchase a burner phone and the cheapest service plan. He barely has enough left for a Whopper.

After eating, Wallace refills his to-go cup and sits back down in the booth at the Burger King inside Walmart. The new cell phone charger is plugged into a wall socket next to his booth.

As he watches the cell phone screen blink away the seconds, he smiles thinking about Josh in handcuffs. After last night's emails, Suspense Publishing should be out of business already. His face abruptly turns fearful. Of course, that means his only source of income is gone. *Shot myself in the foot again!* But this time, there are principles involved more important than money. Sometimes, a person has to do the right thing no matter the cost.

This plan with Lucille had better work or he'd be eating bologna sandwiches at the mission. He calls Lucille's number just to make sure the phone works and then hangs up as soon as it starts to ring. It's a thirty-minute cab ride from Lucille's house to the previous drop in Franklin County, so he waits until 1:45 to call back. He imagines Lucille fumbling for the cell phone in her purse.

"Yeah." Her greeting is not exactly cheerful.

"Don't talk; just listen. Do everything I say immediately. Tell the cabbie to take you to the Walmart on Vine Street."

"What—?"

"Shut up. Don't even think about this. Just do it right now."

Wallace can hear her muffled voice talking to the cab driver.

"Lucille, are you there?"

"Yes."

"Stay on the phone and don't take any other calls. Let me know when you get out of the cab in front of the store. I'll tell you what to do next."

Wallace is watching from Walmart's foyer when a cab arrives and Lucille opens the door with the cell phone in her hand.

"I'm at the Walmart entrance."

"I know. I'm watching your every move. Now, walk into the store and go to aisle twelve. Head to the back of the store."

Lucille whirls looking in every direction.

"Do it now!"

When he sees her stomping towards the entrance, Wallace goes ahead of her to a changing room in men's wear.

"There'll be a sale rack of men's blazers on your right. Tell me when you're there.

"I see it; now what?"

"Love that little skirt, by the way. Does wonders for your figure."

"Get on with this, you son-of-a-bitch. I couldn't stand it if somebody saw me in a Walmart."

Wallace can faintly hear her rancorous voice through the changing room door. He stifles his urge to yell back. "Shut up, bitch. Keep your voice down," he says in a measured voice. "There's a blue blazer lying on top of the rack. Put the money in the vest pocket and hang it back on the rack. Walk back to the parking lot and stay on the phone. Let me know when you're outside the store."

He peeps past the dressing room door and sees her stomping away. Again, he feels himself falling in love with the jiggle of that ass. When she's out of sight, he rushes to the rack of blazers. In the dressing room, he rips open the envelope and kisses two thick bundles of twenties before stuffing them in his pants pockets.

Her voice squeals from the phone. "I'm outside. Now what?" Wallace walks quickly to the foyer and watches her fuming in the parking lot. "What now, you son-of-a-bitch?"

"Face away from the building."

She turns.

"Bend over and lift your skirt. I don't believe you wore panties today."

Lucille spins and glares with fury back at the store. "You bastard—"

Wallace pushes the disconnect button and watches her continue the tirade into her phone. A mother leaving the store clasps her hands over the ears of the little boy beside her who had stopped to gape. After Lucille realizes their call is dropped, she hits a speed-dial number. That would be to the boyfriend who is waiting for them to arrive at the farm in Franklin County.

Lucille rushes back toward the store, probably hoping to spot someone in the entranceway with a cell phone. *Silly women.* Wallace steps into the men's restroom. In a stall, he stomps the cell phone into a mangle and drops it into the commode. He sits on the throne imagining her outside searching the crowd for likely suspects. She wouldn't mingle with the masses at Walmart for long. He'd give her ten minutes to give up and take a cab home.

Another Whopper with a milkshake before walking home would be nice. Almost dinnertime.

Chapter 25

Back at his apartment, Wallace refills his wallet and then stuffs the envelope containing the remaining money between novels on his bookshelf. The envelope is too fat not to create a gap noticeable to an experienced crook.

He pulls out "Moby Dick" and "War and Peace," inserting the bills a few at a time between pages. After stealing these volumes from the library, he had found even the annotations were way too long to actually read. So he had downloaded graphic versions from his favorite online bookstore. The books made good banks, however. He lounges back on his sofa, gloating at his colorful leather-bound collection, imagining Wallace Rose on the spine of "Moby Dick."

The blackmail money coupled with the payment from Suspense Publishing in his PayPal account would cover his expenses for at least three months—if he could fight off the urge to celebrate. He turns on his computer and watches the little clock winding. Time to work on his soon-to-be-famous gift to posterity. He pulls up the file *"Wallace Rose – The Untold Story"* he'd begun the previous day. The title was as far as he'd gotten.

Through the rest of the afternoon, Wallace alternates between sitting in front of his computer and pacing from one side of his tiny apartment to the other. His earlobes are sore from tugging. He finds his Orioles baseball cap stuffed behind a cushion of the sofa and turns the bill sideways on his head, the correct way to stimulate creativity. The Muse is not amused.

Walking to the refrigerator, he stares in at a half-full fifth of Jagermeister, the only alcohol he has left. The Muse might need a shot for a kick-start, but the thought of the licorice taste turns his stomach.

The only trick left to entice the Muse is meditation. He stretches himself on the floor in front of the couch and pulls up his shirt so the third eye that will replace his belly button can see. His body puddles on the floor, as he takes deep cleansing breaths. The mind-clearing "omm ... " chases away conscious thoughts. Starting with his toes and fingers, his limbs become numb and fall away. The window of his soul opens inviting divine inspiration.

The last scene of "A Lovely Murder" begins to play in front of the all-seeing eye. However, the action is different. It's bright daylight rather than night. He's in some character's head looking down at the crumpled body of Stanley, blood oozing from bullet wounds in his chest.

Wallace's eyes pop open. *That's it! The story didn't end right.* The Muse's stories always ended with the bad guy getting shot by the police. The Muse hadn't deserted him after all; just miffed that he'd made up his own ending. Wallace feels loved again. His humming mantra resumes; eyes clinch trying to see more.

He's back in that unknown character's head. There's an agonized scream, a woman naked from the waist down plummeting from a second story window headfirst to the sidewalk. Wallace bolts to a sitting position, his eyes wide. *Who was that?* He had patterned the Denise character on Lucille. He'd imagined Lucille's naked body so often he knew it wasn't her. Wallace rushes to his writing desk while the images are still fresh, confident that the Muse is with him now.

He closes out the memoir that was going nowhere. He'd have to re-write the ending of "A Lovely Murder" before the Muse would help him with something new. But was it already too late? The story was at the publisher. A smug smile creeps onto Wallace's face when he remembers how smart he is. *Suspense* is out of business; Josh bankrupt. Even if Josh were able to publish the story, with this new ending he could change the title and sell it to *Playboy* anyway.

Wallace pulls up the file for the last installment. The Muse is waiting with the changes.

Chapter 26

(Three weeks later)

After settling his bill with Debbie at the reception desk, Dr. Thorn's eleven o'clock patient suggested sarcastically that someone should wake up the doctor to tell him the session was over. Debbie looked in to find him slumped in his chair, chin resting on his chest. She let him continue his nap through the lunch hour. When she knocked loudly and looked in before introducing his one o'clock patient, he hadn't moved. She could see then his eyes were only half closed.

At a hastily called staff meeting, Rachael and the other psychiatrists stared at the conference room table listening to the EMT team a few doors down going through the heart attack revival routine. Debbie, head bowed, eyes closed, announced flatly, "He's dead." No one questioned it or asked for details.

Technically, Dr. Thorn was the head of their psychiatric group. However, over the twenty years since founding Regional Psychiatric Associates, he'd lost interest in administration. Debbie, his Business Manager since the beginning, had taken over the day-to-day decisions, allowing him to lapse into his preferred role as witty curmudgeon. Unlike his colleagues who were over-schooled on the platitudes used by typical therapists, he spoke his mind in plain English. Some patients loved him; others stormed out after the first sessions never to return. Rachael had snickered to herself when she overheard Debbie jumping Dr. Thorn's ass about not acting professionally. Debbie was the hen that ruled the roost.

As they listened to Dr. Thorn being wheeled down the hall on a gurney, Rachael watched the other psychiatrists, all older men with distinguished beards, staring dry-eyed at Debbie like a class of children awaiting their next assignment. A friend's death bounced off them like a rubber ball. Rachael wasn't so much surprised by them as alarmed for herself.

After hiring her fresh out of med school last year, Dr. Thorn had been her mentor and confidant. Since her mother's death, Debbie and Dr. Thorn were her family. Nobody was closer, yet she couldn't cry. A steady diet of other people's calamities emotionally stunted psychiatrists, an occupational hazard as predictable as black lung for a coal miner.

Finally, tears welled in her eyes, not for Dr. Thorn, she realized, but for herself, the inert person she had become. Rachael felt the men glancing furtively her way to see if the *new girl* would wilt. The associate beside her touched her arm and she looked up into a face devoid of empathy, the handkerchief he offered just a rote response to the sight of tears.

For Debbie also, business would take precedence over mourning. Somehow, they'd have to cover Dr. Thorn's patients. As the junior member of the practice, Rachael's caseload was the lightest, so she was the logical choice to pick up the slack. She volunteered to take as many of Dr. Thorn's cases as she could before Debbie got around to asking.

Chapter 27

After the meeting, Rachael asked Debbie to reschedule her appointments so she could start the inventory of Dr. Thorn's office. It seemed eerie to open his office door without knocking first. She longed for his usual jovial greeting. The wrapper of a breakfast burrito and a to-go coffee cup in the trashcan divulged his last meal. She tossed a half-eaten brownie lying on his desks in the trashcan as well and swept the crumbs onto the floor. The janitorial service vacuumed the offices every night.

She dreaded sorting through Dr. Thorn's personal possessions. His apparition seemed to cling protectively to everything. *Do the hard stuff first*, her mother's advice chided in her head. With a sigh of resolve, she circled behind the desk and lowered herself into Dr. Thorn's Oxford leather chair. Her fanny didn't align with the divots Thorn's rump had worn into the plush padding.

The records of Thorn's last patient were still open on the desk. Beside it, his pen rested atop a yellow legal pad. *Electra Complex symptoms manifest* … scribbled at the top was likely Thorn's last thought before the heart attack. Rachael detached the top sheet from the pad and inserted it into the folder before spinning in the swivel chair to the credenza behind to start a stack of cases to be assigned to the other doctors. She definitely didn't want this one.

There was already a folder on the credenza that Dr. Thorn must have been working on before his last appointment. Clipped to the cover was his handwritten memo for Debbie to have his notes typed before adding to the file.

Patient: *Rose, Wallace*
Physician: *Dr. H Thorn*
Date: *20Jun16*

Patient Wallace Rose is a no-show for routine

follow-up on this date. This is the second missed appointment without giving prior notice. Office manager to call the patient one-day prior to next appointment. If patient is again absent, entry will be made in medical record that treatment is terminated due to lack of cooperation. Notice of discharge and final billing to be sent to patient's address and insurance company if applicable. Since follow-up evaluations were a condition of discharge from the psychiatric ward, a notification will be mailed to Police HQ as well. — HT

She thumbed through the rest of the file, ten pages of routine admissions forms and test results. Patient Rose's next appointment was tomorrow. Rachael started another stack of folders for Debbie. If she called Rose and he still didn't show, Rachael could go ahead with the discharge without the need of reassigning the case. *One less loony to deal with.*

A pang of self-loathing bleared her vision and she rose and stood facing the window to hide her face from the room even though there was nobody else present. Her image reflected in the windowpane like a specter, the eyes judging, accusing. It was her mother's eyes.

At what point had these case files become just raw material for the machinery of the hospital, cold words in reports to be sorted and filed away? The eyes became bewildered. Her mother would never understand.

Every day her mother had waited at the door for Rachael to return from work, eager to hear about her diagnosis of a new patient, or how her treatments of the long-term patients were progressing. She knew Rachael's patients who had weekly appointments by name and asked about them with sincere empathy as if they were family members who had fallen on hard times. She wrung her hands in commiseration with every setback or danced in glee if their condition had improved.

It had been easy for Rachael to rationalize the sin of discussing her patients because her mother never left the house and never talked with anyone besides her. Since grade school, when Rachael's father had left them, her mother had suffered chronic depression. Medicine had reduced her sobbing to a manageable catatonic state. As Rachael shared her day over their evening meal, her mother would begin to live again vicariously.

Maybe it had all been for her mother, the lonely years of college and medical training, this nagging drive for perfection. Had she ever really had the desire to heal people, or was that her mother's ambition? Was her infantile need for her mother's approving smile behind it all?

When a heart attack had suddenly taken her mother, Rachael had anticipated a period of mourning. She counseled patients with loss every day and knew it to be unavoidable. It had been Debbie that had detected the onset of something more serious, depression, her mother's disease, and gathered Rachael under her wing.

At first, she had rebelled when Dr. Thorn had approached her about counseling. It would be too embarrassing if the rest of the staff found out. Dr. Thorn had guided her into his office anyway and assured her that half of his patients were other doctors from the hospital, some of them psychiatrists, who he met with discretely. "I won't give you names, but you would be surprised. It seems that tormented minds are drawn into our profession, a belief that they can slay their own demons, perhaps. And considering the stress doctors deal with daily, it's inevitable that the caregivers wind up as the most in need of care."

Debbie and Dr. Thorn had dragged her from the brink of a bottomless pit, a fate Rachael considered to be worse than death. She began to understand the co-dependence that had developed with her mother; why after her mother died she felt incomplete, without purpose. But understanding does not always mean cure.

Her memory drifted back to the warmth she once felt when she connected personally with her patients, her eagerness to use what she had learned to make their lives better. It seemed so long ago although it had been less than a year since she had started practice. That joy seemed out of reach now. It was the memory of a different person that only other people recognized as Dr. Henley.

The stern reflection of her own face glared back from the windowpane now. Her mouth tightened in resolve. She would take back her life and ... And what? She felt adrift on a vast sea, with no point of departure to look back to or any destination in sight. It was a freighting sensation, but also exhilarating. She could loosen herself from the past, like an insect emerging from a cocoon, and a new Rachael could fly free. Any direction she chose would be better than no direction at all.

At five o'clock, Rachael realized she'd only made it halfway through reviewing Dr. Thorn's current patient files. Frustration was turning into panic. She got up again and stretched in front of the window, frowning down at the parking lot below. On top of her current workload, would she have enough energy to make it through this? *Stupid question.* There was no choice but long days, at least until she and Debbie distributed Dr. Thorn's cases and worked through the scheduling conflicts. She'd have to make every minute count. When Debbie came into view walking across the tarmac to her car, Rachael knew there was only one solution. She gathered the remaining yet-to-be-assigned patient folders into a cardboard banker's box. Debbie would have a fit if she knew patient files were being taken out of the hospital, but, under the circumstances, there was no alternative. After dinner, she would finish sorting through Thorn's client files at home. She left the Rose folder on Debbie's desk on the way out.

Chapter 28

After her first appointment the next day, Rachael went back to Dr. Thorn's office to start again. Debbie barged in right after her.

"Wallace Rose won't be coming today."

"He called in?"

"No, he's dead. When I phoned to remind him about his appointment this morning, I got the police department instead. I guess they had his incoming phone calls transferred to the police station. They found him hanging from a ceiling fan in his apartment a couple of weeks ago. Nobody got around to telling us."

"Suicide?"

"Probably, they said, but until they can rule it out, they're treating it as a homicide."

"Murder?" She and Debbie stared at each other, considering what would happen next. This was not the first time for Debbie. Suicide and murder are as routine for a psychiatrist as heart failure is for a cardiologist. But it was the first time for Rachael, and she wasn't looking forward to learning how the game was played.

Debbie picked up on her concern and clarified, "If the coroner had ruled it a suicide, the police would probably want an affidavit summarizing the patient's diagnosis. In a murder investigation, they will probably get a court order for all his medical records. Technically he was still our patient when he died. If you take his case, you'll have to deal with it."

When Debbie tossed the Rose file on the desk, Rachael tried to remember what she'd read yesterday; but it was too jumbled in her head with all the other patient information she'd read last night. "I'll review the file today sometime, but you'd better get me into Dr. Thorn's digital recorder in case there is something that hasn't been transcribed yet. I need to see how all this might look in court, see if the hospital is liable in some way."

Debbie pulled out the center drawer of Dr. Thorn's desk and placed a handheld digital recorder on the desktop. She scribbled a password on a notepad. "There's nothing from Herbert in the transcription queue. I've already checked."

Debbie moved to the door and then stopped with her hand on the knob. "Thanks for volunteering. I know cleaning up after Herbert must be like pouring alcohol onto raw skin for you. If you hadn't offered … Well, I would have had to ask you anyway. I wouldn't trust any of the guys to do this without screwing it up. It works out the same in the end, but you didn't make me feel like such a bitch." Without looking back, Debbie went on through the doorway and missed Rachael's smile.

Despite her hard-as-nails demeanor, Rachael knew Dr. Thorn's death was not easy for Debbie either. Rumor had it that they had been lovers after Dr. Thorn's wife died. Rachael could spot it in the eye contact between them that lasted a little too long and ended with knowing smiles as they shared a common memory. Had they done it on Thorn's desk? With her sitting in his lap in this very chair?

The laid-back Dr. Thorn was the polar opposite of the capital A personality of Debbie. Opposites do attract, however. They may have considered marriage at some point, but both were smart enough to know they could take just so much of each other. Their comfortable friendship and working relationship would have been at risk if they let their bond progress beyond an autumn-of-life fling.

Debbie had never been married. Maybe there had been offers when she was young … maybe not. Even a younger version of Debbie would be intimidating for most men. This is the part that scared Rachael when she thought about Debbie; alone, childless, turning into an old maid married to her work. They were too much alike not to draw the parallel.

Rachael opened the bottom file drawer on Dr. Thorn's desk to use as a footrest and rocked back in his chair, the posture Dr.

Thorn would assume when she came in for a visit between patients. If she concentrated, she should be able to review Rose's medical records in the hour before her next appointment. She worked from the back of the file, the earliest entries, to verify there were no underlying conditions to consider or prior history of mental disorder. The last entry added to the file was a form filled out by hand three weeks earlier by Dr. Thorn.

Patient: *Rose, Wallace*
Physician: *Dr. H Thorn*
Date: *27May16*

Patient is identified as Wallace Rose, 510 Riverside Drive, Bentwood, SC. Admissions form describes Mr. Rose as male, brown hair, brown eyes, height 5' 10", weight 143 pounds, approximately 40 years of age.

Mr. Rose was brought to ER at 10:21 PM 16May16 by ambulance accompanied by BPD Officer Bernard Lewis. Patient incoherent when admitted to ER. Unable to provide personal data, next of kin, or employment status. Name and address obtained from a search of his wallet by the policeman. The officer reported he'd received a call to investigate a disturbance and found Rose in an upstairs apartment hanging by the neck from an extension cord.

ER treated Rose for abrasions on his throat consistent with a power cord and a single hematoma above his left ear believed to have occurred when his head impacted the floor after being cut down. X-rays and examination in ER revealed no additional pathology. ER added additional diagnosis of psychosis due to alleged suicide attempt. Per SOP, he was admitted under a mandatory three-day hold pending further diagnosis.

Mr. Rose currently in residence on the seventh-floor psychiatric ward awaiting examination. Initial screening is scheduled for 10 AM in my office on this date. Because a police investigation is required for an attempted suicide, I am recording the entirety of my meetings with Mr. Rose as well as my verbal conclusions for transcription. Patient will be made aware of the recording, but due to the nature of the case, his permission is not required.

Transcripts to be added to patient's record after my review.

Rachael thumbed through the rest of the forms looking for notes from their meetings. Apparently, this first session and any follow-up sessions with Rose had not yet been transcribed. The recordings, probably several hours of them, would have to be reviewed. She stuffed Thorn's recorder in her briefcase for use later at home.

Chapter 29

Rachael cued up the recorder to Dr. Thorn's first interview with Wallace Rose and sat it on the table in her eat-in kitchen so she could listen while fixing herself something to eat. By the time she had unboxed a frozen dinner, set the microwave timer, and settled on one of the dinette chairs, Thorn was finishing up the standard questions asked all patients sent to the psychiatric ward by ER. Although the questions ask about the patient's background, the primary purpose is to establish for the record that the patient is cognizant and alert enough for the examination.

> *"Mister Rose ... Why are you here?"*
>
> *"Some guy tried to kill me."*
>
> *"No, I mean, why do you think you are in the psychiatric unit?"*
>
> *"Because nobody believes me. The police think I tried to kill myself."*
>
> *"And you didn't try to kill yourself? Why did the policeman not believe you?"*
>
> *"I don't know. I was almost dead when I got to the hospital. I couldn't talk. It hurts to talk now. Can I have some water or something?"*

Mechanical click of the recorder being put on pause.

> *"Now, Mister Rose, can we resume? So, you believe someone tried to kill you?"*
>
> *"You don't believe me either, do you? Well, you can go fuck yourself. I'm through answering questions. Just let me out of this joint. I'll take care of it myself."*
>
> *"Mister Rose, let me explain how this works.*

You were brought in semiconscious last night. The police reported that you attempted suicide. The admitting physician, based on what he observed, initially diagnosed you as psychotic and a danger to yourself. All that may be wrong, but that diagnosis will stand until I change it. I can't release you from the hospital until we've finished this examination."

Sigh followed by a faint sniffle and then a long pause.

"Mister Rose ... ? Mister Rose, maybe we should resume this afternoon. With a little more rest and a nice lunch, maybe you can see I'm trying to help you."

Papers rustle next to the microphone. Dr. Thorn checking his appointment schedule.

"I'll have a nurse bring you back at two, will that be OK?"

A pause again as Thorn waits for a reply and then the click of the recorder being cut off. The afternoon session begins with Dr. Thorn speaking close into the microphone repeating the patient's name, date, and time.

"Mr. Rose. You look much better. Please be seated. I'm told you were able to sleep a little. Things will be much clearer to you now. Just a reminder that we're still recording our meeting, to help me with my notes later."

Sound of pages turning in Dr. Thorn's notebook. Debbie had bought all of the psychiatrists leather-bound notebooks with their names embossed on the front. She insisted note taking fulfilled their patient's stereotype of a competent analyst. Dr. Thorn's notebook only contained doodles.

"You were telling me about your awful experience last night. Can we begin again at that point? You said someone tried to kill you, is that right?"

"And you didn't believe me."

"No, no Mr. Rose.

Rachael imagines Dr. Thorn's wide, ease-the-tension grin.

"I'll need to know more. All I have now is what I read on the admittance—"

"I don't remember much. Just hearing something behind me, and then choking, trying to get that damn noose off my neck. It was that guy, the guy from the café who did it. Must have knocked me out.

"Look at this. Well, you can't see through the bandage, but there's a goose egg."

"Quite a bump. That must have hurt."

"Not at the time. Didn't even know I'd been hit in the head until some nurse poured alcohol on it last night. Felt like a blowtorch. I think I hit her. Did I hit her? I didn't mean ... Man, I'm sorry if I hurt her."

"There is nothing here about a scuffle in the ER, about anybody else being hurt."

"Good. Man, that's a relief. Must have wanted to hit her and then didn't. You know how sometimes you think about doing something, and then later, when you think back on it, you don't know if you actually did it or just thought about doing it. Know

what I mean?"

"Uhh ... I'm not sure that I do. I'll make a note and we'll talk about that later. Maybe now you could tell me about this man that hit you. Do you know him?"

"I call him Stanley in the story. Don't know his real name. I didn't get a look at the guy, but it was Stanley all right."

"Story ... ?"

"I'm a writer. Mysteries. That's how I make my living. Well, I put this Stanley character in one of my stories. He's a real sleaze ball—murdered his girlfriend's husband. I'm the only one that knows he did it; so he's got to kill me, shut me up. That's how it's got to end."

"End ... ?"

"Yeah, the murderer always kills the witness in the end."

"So, a man in this story you made up tried to kill you? Is that what you're saying?"

The recorder was silent for several seconds.

"You don't believe me, do you?"

"It's not important what I believe, Mr. Rose. What's important is that you believe it."

Another pause.

"Well, that's okay. I need to stay here anyway. Nobody gets in or out, right? The food's good, better than I'd fix for myself. So yeah, I guess I'm nuts. I must have tried to kill myself, is that right? I'll try it again if I get out. Yeah, that's what I'll do. I'll use

a gun this time ... I don't have a gun. I'll slit my wrists then. That's not how it's supposed to end, but I can rewrite that part."

"When you are released, you are going to try suicide again?"

"That's it, Doc. You can't let me out or I'll kill myself. I'm paranoid or something ... Schizophrenic—isn't that where you see things?"

"Mr. Rose, don't you think you should leave the diagnosis to me?"

"Sure Doc, I—"

"Please call me Dr. Thorn."

"Yeah, that's it, Dr. Thorn. I'm seeing stuff right now, crawling on the wall, there behind you."

Chapter 30

When the microwave bell dinged, Rachael clicked PAUSE on the voice recorder. As she peeled the cellophane off the Mac-N-Cheese Delight, steam billowed out, scorching her fingers. She was at the sink running cold water over her hand when the muffled sound of her cell phone sent her scrambling to the den, slinging water off her hand and looking for her purse. The caller ID confirmed it was Freddy. She let it go to voicemail.

"Hey, it's me. Just checking to see if you want company tonight. Call me back when you get in."

A glass of merlot, sex, and a good night's sleep were exactly what she needed. The callback icon beckoned, but she decided to wait until after eating to decide. It was already late, probably too late to get herself in a romantic mood. And besides, she still had work to do.

After eating half the mac-and-cheese while standing at the kitchen counter, she carried the recorder to the den and sat it next to her cell phone on the coffee table. Her eyes shifted back and forth between them for a moment and then she called.

"Hey, Freddy. How was your day?"

"The usual. How about yours?"

"Lots of stuff going on. Busy as hell. Dr. Thorn had a heart attack."

"Died?"

"Yeah. Yesterday morning—right in the middle of a session. Everybody's in shock."

"Heart attack, huh. Imagine that? No suspicion of anything else?"

"Hell, I don't know Freddy. How about a little sympathy? He was my friend—yours too."

"Yeah, I was just at his house two days ago. Took him a box of my special chocolates."

"You brought him marijuana?"

"I've got some left. Hows-about me bringing some over and I'll comfort you?"

"Not tonight Freddy. I'm whipped. How about tomorrow night?"

There was a pause, "I've been thinking about you all day. I've got horns a foot long."

She felt blood rush to her face. It wasn't embarrassment, but resentment that he had summarized their relationship in such crass words. No rationalizing "horns a foot long" into something romantic. But this *understanding* about sex had been her idea, her demand. Just skip the starry-eyed courtship of teenagers; no tedious expectations lovers put on each other. Just a carnal arrangement between friends.

"I'd like to, Freddy. I really would. But it just wouldn't happen for me tonight. You'd leave me behind again, more frustrated than I am now."

"I wouldn't—"

"Tomorrow's Friday. I'll take off early. Bring over some Chinese about six. And some of that merlot we picked out together—two bottles. I feel a drunk coming on."

"You got it, Baby Girl."

"And by the way, Freddy, don't call me that.

"How about Sugar Puss?"

"How about Rachael? See you tomorrow."

Chapter 31

Rachael drew herself a half-glass of white wine from the box in the fridge to wash Freddy out of her mind and settled back on the sofa to continue listening to the recording.

> *"Yeah, that's it, Dr. Thorn. I'm seeing stuff right now, crawling on the wall, there behind you."*

Doctor Thorn's chair squeaked. He must have turned to look where Rose pointed.

> *"What do you see?"*
> *"Dragons—with forked tongues and long toenails. They're green. They're coming to get me."*
> *"Mr. Rose, there's nothing there."*
> *"But I see them. Don't you get it? I've got these delusions. They're real to me."*
> *"The only delusion, Mr. Rose, is that you are expecting me to believe your poppycock."*

There was a pause. Rachael imagined Thorn with a stern glare.

> *"Mr. Rose, you were brought in as an attempted suicide. You tell me some character you made up tried to kill you. You obviously need medical help, so there is no need to make up symptoms. That's just going to make my job harder."*
> *"Are you saying I can stay?"*
> *"Yes, you will have to stay … until we get to the cause of your confusion. I have to make a diagnosis and prescribe a treatment. Nothing can happen to you here, so relax. I'm committing you for another*

three days. And, if you and the insurance company agree, maybe you will stay longer."

"There's no insurance company."

"Then how long you stay is entirely up to us. Does that make you feel better, Mr. Rose? But you must quit trying to mislead me. Please, just tell me the truth and we can work through your troubles together."

"But you didn't believe the truth."

"I didn't say that, Mr. Rose ... not exactly—"

Rachael was awakened by the click of the recorder at the end of the session. It was a little after ten on the wall clock in the kitchen. She'd been asleep for over an hour. Have to rewind and start again. But it would have to wait. If she didn't get to bed right now, she'd be a zombie tomorrow.

Chapter 32

The shower warmed up as Rachael undressed. She propped herself stiff-armed on the counter and leaned toward the mirror. *Hazel?* Yes, her eyes were hazel. Freddy had asked if her eye color would be considered hazel. How could she look at herself in the mirror every day and not know her own eye color?

Standing back, she made a deliberate appraisal. Her Mother's sagging breasts. When did that happen? She lifted them to where she remembered and let them fall. Her stomach was still flat, her hips a size four. But it was time to move on—before the flower began to fade.

What next?

Ditch Freddy and look for a suitable marriage, a house in the burbs with an extra bedroom that could be converted into a nursery. One kid—no more. She did the math almost daily. If she became pregnant right now, she would be fifty-five when the child finished college. There might be a few years after that for retirement, before grandkids, before becoming seriously old. This future seemed mapped out, as inevitable as her life to this point had been.

High school dean's list, lead in the school play, head cheerleader her senior year. College went along the same lines. Top ten percent in medical school. Success meant touching all the bases; being perfect. She always paid whatever price was required to win.

But win what? Was there a prize at the bottom of the box? How could she appear so successful, yet feel like such a loser? A bird's eye view of her life was depressing. The total was a novel too predictable to finish. In the end, she would be the best rummy player in some old-folks home.

Only Freddy, or more specifically sex with Freddy, suspended her charge through life. It had only been three weeks since she had literally run into Freddy at a crosswalk in the hospital parking lot. She hadn't seen him before hearing the thump on her fender. After having him checked out at the emergency room, she'd brought him home to dinner as an apology. Things had progressed quickly. He was in her bed the following night.

The illusion of Freddy appeared behind her in the mirror, reaching around with giant's hands to cup her breasts, eyes half shut, ecstasy drawing his lips tight across his teeth. The abandon on his imagined face brought her arousal. Her hands teased her body like Freddy's would do. Their climax would come as a tangle on the tile floor, squirming and giggling in the residue of sex.

A slow-burning gloom crept in to squelch her excitement. Mother would not have approved of Freddy. *With nothing in common, marriage would become a bore,* she would have advised. *When lust wears thin, as it always does with men, he'll seek his pleasures elsewhere. Being happy in the moment is all he cares about. He has no ambition. And you certainly can't expect mister happy-go-lucky to support your career.*

At least that last part she suspected was true. When her latest insecurity at work boiled over into the anxiety of the day, Freddy became the RCA dog with head tilted in confusion. Her foul moods were to be avoided rather than commiserated. Mother was right again. Freddy was a lover, not a potential husband. She'd have to wean herself; plan how to end it without either of them getting hurt. Freddy would be filed away with the other might-have-beens that didn't measure up.

In high school, her girlfriends swooned over their latest boyfriends with whom they had fallen in love. Rachael had suspected this was all theatrics; self-delusions based on romance novels or movies. For her, courtship was simply a contest to find a boy of whom her mother would approve. After a date, her mother would listen, ask questions; and then declare the boy unworthy before ever meeting him.

Later, during her college years, the more suitable the candidate she brought home, the more faults her mother would find. As her mother's dementia progressed, her motives became less disguised. It had never been about the merit of the suitors—or even her daughter's welfare. Her mother's fear of abandonment drove everything. Love, coming from her mother or a man, could not be trusted, a no-win game, a trap to avoid.

As she looked in the mirror, her face had gone from excitement to annoyance, and now was at resolve. She stepped into the shower and closed the sliding glass door. Vapor billowed around her as the water pounded her back.

"Bullshit!" She yelled into the cloud. Listing Freddy's faults might justify her plan for a breakup to her mother, but it was a thin cover. She couldn't get away with dumping this at her mother's feet. She was not in love with Freddy, but there was a raw, overpowering emotion—jealousy. His blasé simplicity was what she envied. For him, there was no haunting past or anxious future. She had tried to allow herself to be transformed by his example, but this tantalizing freedom was out of reach. Instead, she remained a tagalong, an interloper, an orphaned child looking through a candy store window at goodies she couldn't have.

The ambitious sophisticate she would seek out to replace Freddy would not have his free spirit. Both personality traits don't come in the same package. This husband-to-be would be just as anal as she. They would reinforce each other's tedium of regurgitating past triumphs or planning the next steps on their career ladders. Life, actual living, would be the fleeting transitions from past to future.

A shiver overtook her.

Chapter 33

When Rachael turned the corner from the hospital corridor into the Psyche Unit waiting room, Debbie was already making coffee. Rachael pulled out the glass pot and poured all that had run through the coffee maker so far into a Styrofoam cup.

"Going to be awfully strong unless you wait."

"If I had a syringe, I'd mainline." She alternately puffed and sipped trying not to scald her tongue.

"You look tired. Are you going to make it today?"

"You giving me a choice?"

When Debbie chuckled, Rachael couldn't help but join in. It was a relief to hear her laugh. "How about you? Do you need a free session?"

Debbie stared down the hall toward Dr. Thorn's office, the smile suddenly gone. "Maybe … " she said quietly to herself

Rachael tried to imagine the memories that office conjured up for Debbie, clandestine meetings, younger bodies wrapped together in passion.

"You've got my schedule. Drop in between appointments today. We both need to talk."

Debbie waved her hand in front of her face as if shooing off a fly, and then Debbie the business manager was back. "So where are you on Herbert's files? Got anything for me to look at?'

"I'll finish sorting through his open cases this morning. Let's talk again at lunch. I can take on maybe a third of the cases, but the guys will have to do their share."

"Leave that part to me."

"And I'm taking the easy patients. Quite frankly, I'm leaving the degenerates for the other doctors to fight over. That's the one benefit I'm claiming for taking on this project."

"Understand. Believe me, they would do it to you, given the chance."

The coffee maker finally finished dripping. Rachael and Debbie poured full cups to take with them.

"Gotta open us up for business," Debbie said as she walked away.

Rachael pulled a smartphone from her purse and checked her schedule. An hour and a half before the first appointment at nine. Another hour session after that. Nothing else until the afternoon. That gave her three hours to work on Dr. Thorn's files.

She scurried to Dr. Thorn's office, let herself in with a master key, sat in his chair, and then froze as she decided what to work on first. The Rose file was right in front of her, still open from yesterday. She needed to read this right away, but if she let herself start digging into this, she might miss her commitment to Debbie. Her mother chimed in. *Every minute spent planning saves five in execution.* She'd tried to squelch her mother's words of wisdom, the little quips that had been a steady diet growing up, but they flashed unannounced into her head. She swiveled the chair and left the Rose file on the credenza behind the desk to be dealt with last.

First, all of the desk drawers and the doors of the credenza were opened to see if any files had been left out of the file cabinet. Nothing unexpected. The shallow center desk drawer contained trays of assorted pens, paper clips, and gum wrappers. Her pointer finger raked around looking for keys or anything important.

There were three thumb drives. Two were labeled backup in Thorn's scrawl. The third was unlabeled, probably never used. One at a time, she loaded these into Thorn's computer and scrolled through the subfiles. The unlabeled drive contained a manuscript, a not well-written true crime thriller she concluded after scanning a few pages. After the book, there was a porn video, really raunchy threesome stuff. Thorn must have downloaded these from the Internet onto the external drive rather than risk infecting his hard drive. These contents didn't seem to fit with the intellectual Dr. Thorn she knew. Could she remember him mentioning reading for pleasure, or even watching TV? Who really knows someone else's mind, or what they do in private moments?

This shouldn't be left lying around to be discovered by somebody else who might not be so protective of Dr. Thorn's reputation. Rachael dropped the thumb drive on the carpet and ground it with her foot. She couldn't even make a scratch on the hard case. She looked around for something hard to hammer it with, but there was nothing. She considered taking the elevator to the surgical floor and dropping it in one of their red sharps containers but instead flipped the thumb drive into the trashcan. Janitorial would dispose of it along with the rest of the trash tonight.

She turned to the bookshelf of reference manuals above the credenza. There was a thick DSM-6, a string of books by Freud and Jung, all work related, all in plain view to impress the clients. She looked between the textbooks for porn magazines or whatever. There was nothing.

Debbie poked her head in at noon. Sniffing the air, she searched out the apple core and banana peel from Rachael's lunch in the trashcan.

"Come on in. I'm done!" Rachael took a deep breath and smiled. "What now?"

"Let's take all the files to the conference room and lock them up. I'll need to do an inventory to make sure no files are missing before I transfer the cases. We'll have a staff meeting after working hours tomorrow. I'll assign you the cases you've pulled out for yourself first. Then we'll start the donnybrook over who gets the rest. I should be able to beat them into submission by say, seven. Does that work for you?"

"Tomorrow? Yeah, that works. I'm taking off after my three o'clock today. I need a decent meal and some R and R."

"Your boy-toy coming over?"

Rachael stiffened and stared at Debbie counting the file folders stacked on the desk. Debbie had met Freddy at a dinner party at Dr. Thorn's house two weeks ago and they'd seemed to hit it off. But she couldn't know anything other than they were friends—unless Freddy had said something. Who knows what he might have told her.

"Yeah," Rachael said when Debbie looked up.

Debbie arranged the folders alphabetically in a cardboard file box, then moved the patient chair to prop open the door. "Give me a hand?" She backed through the door with her end of the box. "Say hello to Freddy for me. If you didn't have me by twenty years, I'd steal him."

Chapter 34

Rachael turned the key and pushed open the door to her dead mother's house. She hesitated as she gazed into the dreariness. Fibers of dust floated in and out of the slices of light coming through the window blinds. It was like peering into a mausoleum. The over-stuffed sofa with her mother's crocheted arm covers at each end, the throw blanket folded across the back to display the flourish of her mother's initials. The same coffee table books from her childhood were stacked neatly in front. She fought the urge to escape back to her car.

The overhead lights did little to dispel the gloom. It wasn't that she didn't have the money to remodel. Replace the sofa at least, new sectional, all in white leather with brightly colored throw pillows in the corners. She'd found just what she wanted online and then talked herself out of buying it. There was always an excuse to put it off. Or maybe this was still her mother's house; she didn't have permission yet.

Through the archway to the kitchen, the minute hand on the dinner plate size wall clock stuttered to the next digit. Almost five. After a quick shower, there would only be thirty minutes to listen to the Rose tapes before Freddy arrived. Yesterday's fantasy flashed into her mind. Freddy wouldn't mind if she waited until after he arrived for the shower.

She sat the recorder on the kitchen counter so she could listen while setting the table.

> *"You didn't believe the truth."*
> *"I didn't say that, Mr. Rose—not exactly."*
> *"Wallace," Rose said after a moment.*
> *"Pardon?"*
> *"I keep thinking my daddy walked in when you say 'Mr. Rose.'"*

"Okay, Wallace. Is that better? By the way, has your family come to see about you yet? Have you contacted anybody?"

"No, no. There's just me. Everybody died in a fire, way back when I was a kid."

"Oh, I'm sorry Mister ... uh, Wallace.

"Well, I ain't!

The office was quiet. Dr. Thorn must have been thinking how to respond without being offensive.

"What I mean is, me and my stepdad never got along."

"How about your mother?"

"She's dead too. They're all dead."

"No ... I mean, didn't your mother try to protect you?"

"Hell no! She always sided with him. If there hadn't been that fire, I was going to run away."

"Friends? Should we notify your friends; let them know you're okay?"

"Naw. I don't want nobody knowing about this, see. Don't want people getting the idea I'm crazy or something.

Pause

"I'm not crazy, am I Doc?"

"Crazy is not defined in psychiatry, so I can't classify your condition as crazy, or not crazy. But I know what you mean. Do you think you're crazy?"

"There's been some crazy stuff ... But I don't think ... "

"Yes?"

"I want to tell you, Doc. I trust you, see. You're the type guy that can sort all this out for me. But I've got to ask you something.

Pause

"What if while we're talking, you find out I did something wrong, you know, like criminal? You gonna call in the cops? I mean, you wouldn't do that, would you? I mean, doesn't doctor-patient confidentiality take care of that, make what I say secret?"

"Wallace, that's generally true. But there are some exceptions, so I want you to listen very carefully. This is going to be the standard spiel us therapists use to keep the hospital from being sued. If it sounds confusing, ask questions.

"Any discussions of past crimes or wrongdoings are privileged information. It would be unethical for me, as your doctor, to disclose this information to others. The only exceptions are if there is a danger to the public. For example, if you disclose you are a child molester or have HIV, I would have to report that. The only thing that can override this confidentiality is a court order for your medical records as part of an ongoing investigation.

"However, if you discussed plans for future crimes or violence, this would not be privileged. I would be obligated to report it to authorities. For example, if you threatened to murder someone or rob a bank, I would notify the police."

"On 'The Sopranos' the guy talks to his shrink about who he's going to whack next."

"Yeah, I've watched that too. That doctor

doesn't disclose because she doesn't want to be added to the hit list, not because it's ethical or legal. Want to think about this before we continue? I have a copy of the APA Ethics Code if—"

"So, the short answer is that if I tell you I embezzled money, or say, blackmailed somebody, that would just be between us."

"That's right. My job is to help you, not to investigate a crime. The only way it might come to light would be if the police convinced a judge that a court order for your medical records was required to solve a crime."

Rachael pushed PAUSE when she heard the doorbell. Freddy had a key, but she had trained him to ring the doorbell and wait to be let in. This was more in line with the suitor-come-calling image if a neighbor was looking. His hands were full of paper cartons and wine bottles.

"Put them on the counter," she directed. "We'll need to microwave the food a little before we sit down. There's a glass of Chablis waiting for you on the table. We'll open the merlot after we eat."

Freddy leaned forward with a pucker, insisting on a peck before jumping to his assignments. If he didn't have his hands full, he'd have wanted more. She'd have to keep him busy or dinner might get postponed.

"Nuke each carton for thirty seconds, then bring them to me. I feel like eating out of serving dishes tonight. I'll light the candles as well."

Freddy busied himself with the microwave.

"While waiting for you, I was listening to a recording Dr. Thorn made of one of his patient sessions. This is one of the clients I'll be taking over. Do you mind if I continue?"

She didn't wait for an answer and pushed PLAY on the recorder.

> *"OK Doc, I'm gonna start telling you the truth, best I can anyway. It's hard for a fiction writer to tell the truth, you know. We lie for a living.*
>
> *"It's better to tell the truth, Wallace. It will make you feel better."*
>
> *"Maybe I'll tell you some bad things I've done, but I ain't no 'danger to society' like you talked about, so this is all between you and me, right?"*
>
> *"My interest is in diagnosing your medical condition so I can prescribe an appropriate treatment. I'll need to know how you wound up in the hospital. To do this, we will have to be open and honest with each other. Can you do that, Wallace?"*

Rachael imagines Dr. Thorn and the patient staring at each other as he decides.

> *"Wallace, please start from the beginning: I'll stop you if you get into something I'd have to report. Just start at the beginning."*
>
> *"I blackmailed this woman. She and her boyfriend murdered her husband and I found out about it. I couldn't pass up the easy money. Her boyfriend found out who I was and tried to kill me."*
>
> *"Wallace, did you make that up?"*
>
> *"Well Doc, that's exactly what I did. I spotted this luscious blonde that turned out to be Lucille Ballard while eating my breakfast at the River City Café. She was acting creepy. I needed a woman like that for a story I was going to start that day, so I followed her around, to fix her in my mind you*

might say. I started making up this story about her.

"I didn't know who she was at the time, so I named her Denise in the story. And then I discovered that whatever I wrote in the story came true. I wrote about Denise and her lover killing her husband. In real life, that's what Lucille did."

"Wallace, you're not being truthful, are you?"

"Swear to God! It's all right here.

There's a jingle sound in the background.

It's all right here on this thumb drive, the whole story. I make a backup of everything I write. Lucille's a murderer, all right. And she paid me to keep quiet about it."

"Don't bother to take it off the keychain; I don't want it."

"If you want to know what happened, why I'm here, you'll have to read it."

Rachael punched the STOP button and rolled her eyes to the ceiling. "The thumb drive in Thorn's desk! Cut off the microwave; blow out the candles. I've got to get back to the office ASAP before janitorial throws it away. You coming?"

Chapter 35

When Rachael returned home, the front door didn't seem so ominous with Freddy by her side. As she bent over poking around for the key slot in the dark, Freddy pressed against her buttock.

"Quit it, you dog!"

"I wish I were a dog. You ever watch dogs doing it?"

She pushed back hard with her rump, "Get out of the light."

He followed her into the kitchen, right behind her every step as she reheated the paper containers of Chinese in the microwave; two minutes for the chow mien, then one minute each for the spring rolls. Steam condensed against the glass door. His lips were wet and smeary on her neck. An elbow to his stomach backed him up for only a moment.

Yes, she'd watched dogs doing it. Every kid secretly watched dogs doing it. The nuzzling, the snapping back, the quickness of it after the bitch's body had been made ready. It was disgusting to feel her body reacting to his touch. "Give it a break. I need to eat."

When the groping suddenly stopped, she looked over her shoulder at him slumped dejectedly in one of the dinette chairs, eyes averted. She rattled in a drawer and handed him a corkscrew. "Make yourself useful." He opened the merlot and poured goblets half full. When he looked up, his eyes cringed expecting her to snap a new demand.

She straddled his legs and lowered herself onto his lap, hugging his face between her breasts. The microwave beeped insistently, the spicy smell seeped out. "I've got something I want to show you." She hopped up and dragged him to his feet. "It's in the bathroom, come on," she said pulling him along. As she looked back, his startle changed to a hearty grin. If he had a tail, it would be sticking straight up and wagging.

They both slumped in dinette chairs while their meal heated up for the third time. Refills of wine sat in front of them untouched. It was too late to keep a buzz alive. Another drink and the yawning would begin.

Freddy's elbows propped on the table, chin cradled in his hands. Half-lidded eyes watched blankly as the food spun in the microwave. Comb marks separated his wet hair into parallel furrows. Ears, normally buried in lush hair, stuck out like on a Mr. Potato Head.

"Freddy ... " She needed to tell him, to get on with the breakup. But you just can't *Whew!* after sex and start right in with *by the way* ... How to word this exactly? Just lay it out there would be best. She needed a husband, and he wasn't on the shortlist. He might just agree. *Marriage? Hell no. If you're planning something permanent, count me out.* That would probably be all there would be to it. *Slam bam, no thank you ma'am.* Might be as simple as that.

"What's wrong, Babe?" Alarm was on his face.

Tears were dripping off her chin. "Freddy ... " Again, she couldn't make herself say it.

"You OK?" Apprehension was turning to panic.

"I don't know—" An uncontrollable sob cut her short. She pressed palms into her eyes and held her breath until it stopped. "I'm just tired." Did she really use her mother's code phrase for: *I'm sparing you my full-fledged panic attack.*

"Did I do something?" The contradictions of words and body language always unnerved men, the reaction her mother would shoot for.

"Freddy, do you love me?"

His face was beyond panic now. All four-letter words were permitted in their private conversations except the L-word. He knew something bad was about to happen. She forced a reassuring smile. The breakup would likely turn messy and she just didn't have the energy left to deal with it right now.

"Freddy, would you stay over tonight? I need your help."

He still looked suspicious.

"You know that thing that you told me you want me to do more than anything in the world?"

He seemed confused for only a second and then his eyes went wide.

"I've been thinking about that too. I'm thinking that should be your reward if you help me with some work tonight."

Chapter 36

Freddy followed Rachael into the bedroom and watched her clear off space on the nightstand for the voice recorder. She plugged the power cord into a wall outlet and then inserted the jack for the earbuds.

"I've got to finish listening to Thorn's recording of this session before tomorrow." She rushed back into the living room and came back with her laptop. "I need you to read what is on this thumb drive. It should be some kind of fiction story the patient was writing. You can give me the *Reader's Digest* version in the morning. I can't do both. Understand?"

Freddy nodded, but he clearly didn't like it.

"I'll be most grateful—in the morning."

After brushing her teeth, Rachael came out of the bathroom wearing flannel pajamas. Freddy was already propped against the headboard reading on the laptop. She slipped under the cover and inserted the earbuds, slapping back Freddy's wandering hand before selecting the PLAY button.

> *"Anyway, I found out this Lucille Ballard was the woman I'd been following. Randolph Ballard, her husband, was murdered that same night, supposedly killed during a home invasion. You must have heard about it; it was all over the news."*
>
> *"Randolph Ballard, president of Citizen's Bank? Played golf with him. Seemed like a stand-up guy. So, you think his wife killed him?"*
>
> *"The police went along with the home invasion ploy, but I thought she and her lover did it. So, I sent her this email about having proof ... pictures or something. That's how the blackmail got started."*
>
> *"Are you still blackmailing her?"*

"Hell no! She and the boyfriend know who I am now, so I'm just trying to stay alive. I'll have to move out of state and change my name or something."

"They found out you are the blackmailer?"

"Yeah. Yesterday I walked into this café in Old Town where I get my breakfast. I picked up the paper and was reading the headlines while walking back to my table. When I looked up, there she was, Lucille, staring me right in the face. The boyfriend was there too, sitting with his back to me. The paper fell right out of my hands.

"I backed up and sat at the counter. When I glanced over, she was still watching me and whispering to the boyfriend. She must have remembered me from that first time I saw her at the café and started putting things together.

"Vera, the waitress, brought me coffee and then started a fuss. 'Wallace,' she says, 'you ain't sticking me with breakfast again. Do you want your regular breakfast or not?' She's a real bitch. The boyfriend turned around and looked my way.

"I couldn't get outta there fast enough, but it was already too late. When I glanced back through the glass front, the guy was at the counter talking with Vera. The bitch probably told him where I live."

"You should contact the police."

"What? And confess to being a blackmailer? Are you kidding? Me and the cops don't exactly get along. I've sorta got a history. I'd wind up in jail for sure.

Pause

"You won't report anything, will you?"

"If I believed you, I might."

"Swear to God and hope to die!"

"Calm down, Wallace. You're distraught right now, not seeing things clearly. Things are getting distorted in your mind. The usual case is that the eye sees something and sends signals to the brain and that becomes reality. But under stress, sometimes it works the other way. The brain sees something and sends that signal to the eye. These are hallucinations; they become your reality. Do you understand?

"I know this murder business seems real to you. All this is perfectly understandable considering what you've been through. It's not so important what you see when your brain is in this state, but why. Our brains are constantly trying to make sense of the conflicting information around us. When the brain gets confused, we become anxious and paranoid. We start to imagine conspiracies, people coming to get us. But you need to understand that it's not real, Wallace. It's just your brain on overload. Understand?"

"But Doc—"

"You trust me, don't you Wallace. I only want the best possible treatment, so you can be well again. If we relieve this stress, your hallucinations will go away ... your paranoia as well."

"But Doc—"

"Don't worry. We can get you back to normal. I'm going to put you on a tricyclic, a pretty high dosage. You can start it tonight. It will calm your brain, alleviate the anxiety you are experiencing. You will feel better right away, but it may take a week or so before it's fully effective. You should stay in the hospital overnight, to see if you have a

*reaction. If there's no adverse side effect, you can go
home in the morning. You want to go home, don't
you Wallace?"*

"But Doc—"

"You'll need to come back weekly.

Rustling of Dr. Thorn's appointment book.

*"Can you come in on Tuesdays at ten? We'll
talk more then, see if your symptoms have subsided.
May need to adjust your dosage.*

*"I'll walk you out to the Nurse's Station.
They'll take you back to your room. Can't have
patients wandering the hall alone on the seventh
floor."*

Background noises in Rachael's earbuds suddenly went silent.
Dr. Thorn had stopped the recorder.

Chapter 37

"Come and get it!" Rachael yelled from the kitchen.

Freddy, still in boxer shorts, moseyed through the doorway scratching his crotch. Puffy eyes showed through sandy ropes of hair wilted over his face. His bottom lip pooched out in a pout.

"Pancakes, with strawberries and whipped cream, your favorite."

"Not fair."

"Isn't this what you're always wanting?" She turned back to the stove to hide her laugh.

"You know what I want. This is not fair."

"Freddy, if you always get what you want, there'll be nothing to look forward to. What did you learn from the memory drive?"

"Maybe I won't tell you."

"Lighten up. Tomorrow's Friday. We can have the whole weekend together if you want. You never know what might happen."

He looked doubtful and plopped down at the kitchen table to mope. "It's just one of those who-done-it mysteries. I guessed who the murderer was before the end."

"Was there a girl character named Denise?"

"Yeah, that was her name—Denise."

"And her lover murdered her husband?"

"Yeah. If you've already read it, why make me do it?"

"I got that from Dr. Thorn's voice recorder. Just checking to see if it matches up." Rachael brought him a cup of coffee and sat across the table. "You know what I think? The story you read is true. Remember a few weeks ago, that bank president that got murdered in his own home, his wife raped? They've never caught anybody."

"You think Herbert's patient is a murderer?"

"Dr. Thorn's patient was also killed, just after he wrote what you read last night. No, he didn't murder the bank president, but maybe he knew who did. That's why he was killed."

"You're talking crazy. You're letting your imagination run wild. If you think there was a murder, then turn everything over to the police. Let them sort it out."

"Not unless there's a court order. Doctor-patient confidentiality applies."

"You said the Wallace guy is dead."

"Same rules apply after death."

"Holy shit, Sherlock. Did it ever occur to you that I ain't no doctor? As soon as you tell the judge I knew all about this, they'll throw me in jail for withholding evidence, accessory after the fact, or whatever." Freddy got up and stomped to the silverware drawer. When he returned, he stood behind her running his fingers through her hair. "Thanks a lot, Rachael. Maybe they'll allow conjugal visits in jail. Maybe we should get married so we won't have to testify against each other."

Rachael twisted to look up at Freddy with an enticing smile intended to defuse his sulk. "Now whose imagination is getting the best of them?"

He grinned back, but she thought it hid anger. His feelings were hurt.

He walked around to the other side of the table and sat before his plate. "Yeah, I've got imagination." He began cutting the pancakes into bite-sizes with the knife he had brought to the table. "The pancakes are nice, but I don't like being treated like a fool." His wide grin contrasted with the harsh tone of his voice. Rachael didn't know which to believe.

"I've got to work out of town for a few days," he said. "Let me borrow that voice recorder and I'll let you know if your theory holds water."

"Freddy, I can't do that. I've already broken more rules than I could explain to an Ethics Committee." She laughed, trying to get him to laugh with her, but his taciturn grin remained.

Chapter 38

Sharing the bathroom with Freddy put Rachael behind. After Freddy left, she'd wasted more time looking for the thumb drive that had been in her computer. Freddy must have absentmindedly put it in his pocket.

She barely made it to the office in time for her nine o'clock appointment, a pimply-faced teen brought in three days earlier by his hysterical mother. His father had taken away his Gameboy due to poor grades. According to the father, the youth had added the suicide threat to his usual tantrum because his mother wouldn't intercede.

As in their previous session, the little turd ignored her and sulked. She made a half-hearted attempt, but secretly hoped he would spare her his harangue of "stupid parents." He was obviously narcissistic, the opposite of the self-loathing depression that led to suicide.

After the session, she met with the terrorized parents and explained in antiseptic terms their son's condition. She avoided the words *spoiled brat* and *manipulative* as they were not recognized terms in the profession. However, she did explain that he would be released today. State law prevented the hospital from holding patients against their will past three days unless diagnosed as a physical threat. In her estimation, he was no threat—at least not to himself.

After escorting the family to the waiting room, Rachael rushed back to Dr. Thorn's office. Debbie knocked on the door and charged in before she got seated.

"There's a detective in the waiting room with a court order for the Wallace Rose medical records. I'm making copies of the file right now. He wants to talk with the assigned physician."

"Did you tell him Dr. Thorn is dead?"

"Yes, of course, but he wants to talk with whoever took over the case. Do you want me to show him in?"

"Yeah, I guess so. Give me five minutes to prepare."

When Debbie left, Rachael propped her forehead on her palms and stared at the desk. The file Debbie was copying did not contain Dr. Thorn's sessions with Rose. These had not been transcribed yet. It was in these sessions that Rose had talked about his writing. Nobody but she, and now Freddy, knew about the thumb drive containing his fiction. There should be no reason for the police to think Wallace's death was anything other than the suicide of a mental patient; nothing to connect Rose to the murder of Randolph Ballard. Might be better to leave it at that for now and let it all blow over. No need to confuse a routine investigation with her speculation. She would just answer the detective's questions without elaborating.

Debbie knocked and let in a rumpled middle-aged gentleman, a brown felt hat in one hand and the file Debbie had just made in the other. His outdated wide tie flared across a paunch. Rachael came around the desk with her hand thrust forward. He stuffed the file under his sweaty armpit to shake.

"Good morning. I'm Dr. Rachel Henley." She motioned to the chair usually occupied by clients. "Please, sit down."

"Detective Duffy. If you can spare a minute, I have a few questions." He smiled broadly and collapsed heavily into the chair.

"We'll take as long as you need. After Herbert—Dr. Thorn died, this case was transferred to me, but I never actually met Mr. Rose."

Duffy held up the file. "You know what's in here?" and then opened it on his lap and started shuffling through the documents. "These medical terms—like a foreign language. Maybe you could just summarize it for me."

"Well, Dr. Thorn diagnosed Mr. Rose with depression and mild psychosis. These are chronic conditions we usually don't treat on an inpatient basis. He was prescribed doxepin, an antidepressant, and scheduled to receive outpatient follow-up weekly with Dr. Thorn. However, he never returned.

"Doxepin? That's it exactly. That's what the lab said he had in his system when he died. Enough to kill a horse, they said."

"So, Mr. Rose overdosed on his prescription and then hanged himself in case it didn't work?"

"No, no, Dr. Henley. Wallace Rose didn't have any in his blood. There wasn't even a prescription bottle found in his apartment. It was Dr. Thorn that had taken a massive dosage of doxepin."

"Dr. Thorn ... ? There must be a mistake. Dr. Thorn would never have taken doxepin. With his heart arrhythmia, even a normal dosage might have caused a heart attack."

"Lab told me that too. How well did you know Dr. Thorn? Was he into recreational drugs? Maybe he'd become addicted?"

"Of course not. Besides this drug won't make you high and it's not addictive."

"Might he have taken an overdose on purpose, to commit suicide?"

"No, out of the question. We're in a psychiatric ward. If he had been depressed or suicidal, a half-dozen people would have picked up on it. When I talked to him the day before his death, he was in top spirits."

"Well, where does that leave us then?"

Rachael couldn't sit any longer. She wandered to the window and looked between the slats of the Venetian blinds at the parking lot below. *Thorn murdered?* It just seemed so absurd. She thought back to their last conversation. Had she missed something? Was he depressed over his heart condition? Maybe there had been more pain than she knew about.

"Doctor?"

She turned and studied the detective's face. His smile remained constant, patiently waiting for her reply. "This is just such a shock.

He was a close friend. I don't know what to think. Is this a murder investigation?"

"Guess I've got two murder investigations now. Neither has been officially labeled as homicide yet." He chuckled. "Not often I get to investigate two unrelated murders on the same trip. Odd that you are a witness for both, don't you think?"

His disarming smile faded to a rigid stare. It was clear this was not an off-hand remark. Why couldn't he just ask yes-or-no questions he could jot into a little book and then go away? He watched her with practiced patience—asking nothing, offering nothing.

"I want to help, but I really don't know anything."

"But you suspect something. Am I right?"

"It's just conjecture. You deal in facts."

A silent chuckle jostled his bulky body. "A good guess is more than I have right now."

Rachael sat back behind her desk, pulled out the center drawer, and laid the copy of Wallace's thumb drive she had made and Dr. Thorn's voice recorder on the desktop. "There's more than what's in that file."

The detective's eyes grew harsh.

"I wasn't holding out. Your court order is for the medical file and that's what you got." Rachael pointed to the items on the desk. You need to know there is information in addition to the file. The voice recorder contains therapy sessions not yet transcribed. It's mostly the patient rambling on, feeling sorry for himself. Probably nothing significant, but you can be the judge of that. This external memory contains a fiction story that Wallace was writing. He gave a copy to Dr. Thorn."

"Fiction story?"

"Wallace was a writer, mystery stories for magazines, that sort of stuff. Again, it probably doesn't mean anything."

Detective Duffy pushed out of the chair and stood before her looking back and forth between her and the two items before picking them up. "What's the bottom line?"

"Honestly, I don't know. I didn't know Wallace Rose, but if someone murdered Dr. Thorn, I want to help all I can."

The detective stared into her eyes, his face slack, as if his body had been put in neutral while his mind worked. "Come to the station on Westcott at eight-thirty Monday." His smile came back. "I'll have the coffee waiting. Don't let it get cold."

"I have patients on Monday morning."

He was already opening the door. "Eight-thirty."

Chapter 39

After walking into the lobby of the Dixie Hotel, Rachael rushed to the restroom. The padding in her bra had shifted causing her breasts to point obliquely. She locked the door before making adjustments. The face in the mirror behind the lavatory startled her, and then she smiled. Her wig was obviously a wig, at least to another woman. The bangs covered down to her cat-eye sunglasses. She turned from side to side, checking the rest of the disguise she had put together at the Goodwill. Satisfied her own mother wouldn't recognize her, she sauntered back across the lobby toward the registration desk. Her hips swayed in exaggeration as she worked herself into character.

"I'd like a room, please," she told the skinny, balding clerk. She'd used her professional voice rather than the sultry voice she'd been practicing and immediately corrected herself. "Any room in the inn?"

The clerk looked at her suspiciously. "I ain't seen you in here before."

"Reckon not. Up from Atlanta for the weekend. Been told this is where the action is."

"That what you've been told?" The clerk's eyes grazed over her like hungry hands.

"See anything you want?"

"Maybe later, if you're still here when the bar closes. You renting by the hour or by the night? If you're planning on renting by the hour, there may not be anything available when you need it."

"One night, maybe two if things turn out." She attempted a flirting smile. The clerk grinned back.

"Fifty in advance."

"Sort of short on change right now. Can you give me a couple of hours?"

"In advance. You know how it is."

Rachael was only guessing *how it is* based on what she'd learned from a prostitute she'd treated for heroin addiction. The clerk was buying it, however. It surprised her how easily the sophisticated persona of Dr. Henley could morph into an uninhibited sex worker. *Which one is the charade?* The clerk's eyes followed expectantly as she fished a fifty out of her bra. She wiped beads of sweat off the tops of breasts with the bill before handing it over.

Walking into the bar after the glare of the lobby was like entering a cave. Only an hour after sunset and the bar stools were already half occupied—all women. She ordered a vodka tonic.

"Want liquor?" The bartender was a burly crew cut guy who must double as the bouncer. Rachael didn't know how to answer so just stared back.

"Give her the real stuff, Tucker. Put it on my tab." A bosomy woman, well painted with rouge, glanced at her sideways from the next stool. Tucker went away to mix the drink.

"You're sort of new to this, I'm guessing. Most of the girls don't drink, you see. Tucker will give you straight tonic water for a dollar. If the john buys you a drink, it'll still be tonic water, but he'll charge five bucks. Tucker takes a cut, of course. He keeps a tab and you settle up at the end of the night."

"You found me out pretty quick. This is all new to me—as a professional I mean. Thanks for the tip."

"I'm Macbeth." She glanced around the room. "I may be the only professional in here. What's your name, Hon?"

"Rachael."

"Is that what you go by or is that your real name?" Macbeth chuckled at Rachael's reaction. "It's OK. Everybody's got to start sometime. You look like a Babs to me. Does that suit you?"

"Macbeth, I'm scared to death. I don't know what I'm doing."

"Look around. Take a close look at the gals. What do you see?"

The women were younger than Rachael had expected, sitting with empty barstools between them, staring into empty drinks or secretly sizing each other up. Some appeared bored, others as angst-ridden as her.

"You're not the only newbie. Most of these girls don't make a living at this. I'm suspecting that's not why you're here either. Some are here to pick up a little egg money while the old man is off on his fishing trip. Some are here to get some excitement they're not getting at home. That one in the booth," Macbeth motioned discreetly with her eyes at a blonde staring at the door, "is a nympho. So eager to jump into bed she won't even charge, I bet. I'm hoping you're not one of them. Hard to compete with free pussy."

"I'm going through a divorce. I am more horny than broke, I admit."

"Well, you'll get your fill here. The regulars always scout out the fresh meat first. We'll get you lined up with the first good-looking stud that walks in. You'll be over your jitters in no time."

"Hello, Macbeth." A familiar voice came from behind their stools. Macbeth twisted around, but Rachael froze.

"Why if it ain't Fred. We were just talking about you. How's it hanging?"

"Around my knees, as usual."

"Be careful. Get that thing excited and it might poke your eye out."

Rachael hunkered over her drink, her hands to the sides of her face as if shielding against glare.

In the mirror behind the bar, Rachael watched Macbeth walk Fred away from the bar and put an arm around his shoulder. She talked into his ear as they took turns glancing at Rachael's back. In the dim light, Rachael thought the guy resembled Freddy. However, his hair was pulled back into a ponytail. Freddy wouldn't be caught dead in a ponytail. And the black blazer and turtleneck were not Freddy's style, but ... Terror caused her ears to roar. She covered her face with both hands. *Stanley!*

Rachael jumped when Macbeth put her hand on her shoulder. "Honey, you're shaking like a leaf."

In the mirror, Rachael searched the room and was relieved Fred was gone. A murderer had been standing right behind her. A shiver overtook her, and Macbeth gave her a reassuring squeeze.

This plan to play private eye had grown after Detective Duffy had left her office this morning. She had reread the copy of Wallace's "A Lovely Murder" that she had downloaded to her computer. If Wallace had patterned the character Stanley on the actual murderer, he must live at the old Dixie Hotel, or at least frequent the bar. Wallace's physical description might be enough to pick him out. She owed it to Dr. Thorn to find out if her hunch was right.

Her mother would cringe in her grave if she knew where her daughter was. Debbie would chide her recklessness. It had been defiance, her rejection of the mousy, neurosis-ridden Dr. Henley that had brought her here. And her plan had played out like a big adventure until … All her bravado had dissolved in an instant. She jerked to her feet and grabbed her purse, preparing to bolt for the door.

"Look," Macbeth said with a compassionate smile. "Fred's a nice guy. I told him about you being new, scared and all. Made him promise to play nice."

Rachael stood petrified, staring in the mirror at their reflection, two garish hookers. Clear-minded reason wrestled with panic. Even if Fred were the murderer, he wouldn't know who she was. He couldn't know why she was here.

"It's understandable being nervous the first time out." Macbeth chuckled. "You wouldn't be the first girl who changed her mind." Macbeth waited again for a response and then gave another squeeze. "I'll leave you alone then. Don't want to talk you into something you'll regret later. If you decide to stay, Fred's room is 213. He's expecting you."

Chapter 40

When Rachael raised her fist to knock, a cacophony of voices screamed in her head, deriding her stupidity, pleading for her to turn and run. She looked down the dimly lit hall to the stairway, then back at the door that separated her well-ordered life from impetuous madness. Even as her internal debate raged, her knuckles rapped the door. At that instant, she felt the earth jolt into its correct orbit and the voices fell silent. There had never been a choice, she realized. Although her fate was unknown to her, it was none-the-less predetermined.

"Fred? Fred, it's Babs."

"Yeah, Babs, come on in," came the muffled voice through the door.

Rachael cracked the door a few inches. "I brought up a pint of whiskey." She stuck the bottle through the opening. "Macbeth said you liked Wild Turkey. I'm fond of it myself." She was going for farmer's-daughter's-first-trip-to-town with her new voice.

She swept the wall inside the door until she found the light switch and cut it off.

The bed banged angrily against the wall when he sat up. "What the—?"

"Please, please, purty please. I'm awful shy. I don't think I could pull my clothes off with a man watching."

"Well … If that don't beat all. I like to see what I'm getting."

"You can see with your hands, can't you? That's what my husband—my ex-husband does."

"See with my hands … ?" He laughed raucously.

Rachael felt relief that this was not Freddy. Freddy never laughed out loud. This voice was self-assured, in contrast to Freddy's meek mumble.

The bed frame squeaked as he lay back. "Yeah, I suppose I can at that. Come on in. Can you find the bed?"

Rachael eased open the door. There was just enough light from the neon signs out front leaking through the pull-down window shade for her to navigate across the creaking floor to the single bed. She screwed off the top of the whiskey and nudged his shoulder. Rainbow colors glinted off the bottle as he tipped it to drink. She undressed. The chill of the room caused her to tremble, even though perspiration ran in rivulets down the small of her back.

He touched her leg with the bottle and she jumped. "Here, have some courage; I won't hurt you."

He waited patiently as she crawled under the cover beside his already naked body. His skin felt ablaze against the coolness of hers.

She waited for groping hands, squeezing, probing. Finally, she sought him out with her hand, and still he didn't move. She felt so naive. How would an experienced prostitute do this? What does he expect? The quietness of the room rang in her ears.

She tried to tempt his body onto hers, and when he wouldn't budge; she straddled him and guided him in. He laid motionless, arms by his sides. In the stillness, she felt his heartbeat thumping inside her, the heat of him kindled embers into flame; flesh began to melt and flow like candle wax.

Rumbling, distant at first, an approaching storm. And then a tempest struck, sweeping her in surging torrents, writhing, gasping for breath. Thunder roared in her ears masking thought. Nothing survived the frenzy except the incessant yearning. Lightning struck. His body stiffened, he gasped, a moan. Lightning struck again, blasting her into another realm where she floated weightlessly.

She collapsed on top of him, her lips greedily searched out his, tongue thrusting, seeking to be inside him as he was inside her. When all energy was finally exhausted, her body lay limp. Comingled sweat and ejaculate welded them seamlessly together.

Long after his breathing steadied in sleep, she studied the neon flickers leaking past the window shade onto the ceiling tiles. Her body still throbbed. Who was this man? Freddy couldn't turn her into a wanton animal that way. Until now, she hadn't known there was an animal.

She glanced to her side at the shadowy profile of his face and smiled. His foreplay had been less than enthusiastic. She had made love to him. Motionless below her, he had somehow controlled her like a dancing puppet. Freddy would have tried all manner of manipulation seeking that response.

Rachael thought back to the nymphomaniac downstairs Macbeth had pointed out earlier. With her tailored dress and styled hair, she was obviously a poodle in a pen full of hounds. Yet she faced the lobby, more eager than the rest to charm the next man who walked in. Had she become addicted to the infusion of adrenaline that accompanied nefarious sex with strangers?

Rachael imagined this woman with two incompatible personas she kept sequestered from each other, each identity derisive of the other's lifestyle when it was in sway. Tomorrow this woman might sit on the terrace of the Ritz with her society friends gossiping over high tea, oblivious to her alter ego downstairs.

Rachael also felt herself ripping apart. Babs was a whore; a body purchased in a shady bar. Her purpose was unambiguous, her worth a direct measure of some anonymous man's pleasure. Rachael's education and achievements meant nothing in this world. Babs' reward was crumpled twenty-dollar bills left on a nightstand. But was it as simple as that? Was it Babs or Rachael who wanted to wake this man, pleasure him again, ascend with him into rapture?

Rachael was surprised these thoughts didn't disgust her, this easy acceptance of Babs the whore as herself. Could Freddy be divided this way also, the gullible innocent in one instance and a remorseless murderer the next? None of this seemed real anymore, as if Fred and Babs were a fantasy existing only in the alternate reality of the Dixie Hotel—all mere imagination.

She repeatedly dozed and then startled awake, her heart racing from fleeting images of violence or passion. Wallace Rose's words to Dr. Thorn echoed to her mind: *It's the only way the story can end. The murderer must kill the only witness.* She imagined the dispassionate eyes as he strangled her when he discovered her identity. The scene replayed in her head like a script the actors were forced to repeat over and over until it was perfect.

She should ease out of bed and creep barefooted to the door. She could grab her clothes and dress in the hallway. It was the only plan. But when he turned in his sleep to face away from her, she continued to lie still—as if some enchantment had rendered her powerless.

Sunrise began to backlight the window shade and lighten the room. He began to stir before waking. She turned onto her side facing away from him and pulled the sheet over her head. Maybe he would just throw money on the bed and leave. The mattress shook as he swung his feet to the floor. He peed and flushed with the bathroom door obviously left open. Terror rose as he stood beside the bed. She tried to control her breathing, appear asleep. She waited for his touch, his command.

The bed jostled as he sat on the corner to dress. Shoes shuffled across the floor. A keyboard clicked. It stopped and then began again. The door opened with a creak and then clunked shut. Footsteps receded in the hallway.

Slowly she peeked from under the cover before jumping to the door to lock it. This was the first time she'd seen the room. On a table beside the window, a laptop was open. A hundred-dollar bill lay on the keyboard. A banner scrolled on the screen: "Bringing back coffee."

She raised the window shade. Below Fred came out of the foyer and walked away on the sidewalk. His hair was stretched back in a ponytail held by a rubber band. She raised the lower window sash and leaned out to watch. Bare ankles flashed above his loafers. He was the murderer Wallace described; the murderer was Fred. Fred was Freddy. It seemed preposterous, but she couldn't convince herself it wasn't true.

Across the street, movement caught her attention. A bulky man got out of a white sedan. Looking down, she couldn't see his face past the brim of his hat. His head turned toward the Dixie, and she jerked back inside.

Rachael needed to escape quickly, but if she were recognized it would mean the end of her career. Babs needed to be seen leaving. The disguise was required one more time. Nobody could ever know Dr. Henley was here.

Her panties were lost somewhere under the bed. She didn't need them anyway and began pulling the dress over her head. As she maneuvered the waistline of the dress past her breasts, she stopped suddenly with a gasp. She'd seen that rumpled brown felt hat before. *Detective Duffy!* He'd read Wallace's story off the thumb drive and had come to the same conclusions about finding the killer at the Dixie.

She rushed back to the window. The man from the car was walking on the far side of the street in the direction Fred had gone. If Fred were headed to that café Wallace mentioned in the story, maybe she could get there by different streets. If she ran all the way, she could get there in time to warn him.

She froze with her hand on the doorknob and then backed away, stunned by what she had been thinking. The cold frame of the computer nudged her bare bottom. By instinct, she fingered ENTER on the keyboard, and the banner flicked away. Icons popped onto the screen indicating the computer was not password protected. She directed the arrow over the word processor icon and thumped twice on the touchpad. *A Lovely Murder* loaded onto the screen.

This was Wallace Rose's computer! Duffy hadn't mentioned finding a computer at Rose's apartment. She rapidly scrolled down. Rose had utilized the change-tracking feature of the software, so his last updates were highlighted. There were only typo edits until she reached Episode 4. Rose had completely rewritten the last installment of his serial.

Chapter 41

A LOVELY MURDER – Episode 4
(rewrite)

Perspiration beaded on Denise's cheeks as she waited for the cab in front of Armand's. She fought the urge to wipe, which would cause her makeup to smear. Her sundress clung to her legs. She wanted to scream, and stomp and curse, but she would have to hold in her misery until she got home.

When the cab pulled to the curb, James rushed to open the door. James—bless his soul—was her only loyal friend left. He offered his arm for support as she entered the backseat. She puckered an air- kiss while pushing a twenty into his palm.

"Please come again for dinner tomorrow, Ms. Ballard. I so look forward to seeing you."

The cab pulled into traffic before she could think how to respond. No, she finally decided. She couldn't continue to come here every night to eat alone. Her girlfriends had found convenient excuses not to join her after her first two invitations. Even Myra avoided her calls, refusing to be drawn into consoling the widow again. Denise always insisted they stay with her for the dancing afterward. Married women couldn't get away with that every night. If she stayed late by herself, the old coots, the Casanovas that hung around, would be asking her to dance, hitting on her like a common pickup.

She was fuming when the cabbie looked at her in the mirror asking with his eyes for her to give an address.

"Take me to the Dixie Hotel."

The cabby's gaze went to the road and then back to her in the mirror, his eyes still questioning.

"The Dixie … ? Do you know where it is?"

"Yes Ma'am I do," he called back to her. "Do you? That's no place for a lady."

"Shut up and drive."

Stanley would be mad, but she was mad, too. He'd have some logical excuse why he'd not met her at Armand's as planned, make her feel like a dope. He wouldn't yell; he was not the yelling type. He'd probably hit her, or maybe he'd be glad to see her. Either way, she had to get this over with.

Denise pushed straight through the swinging doors and upstairs to Stanley's room. She knocked lightly at first, then louder. She tested the doorknob. The door was locked. She had a key but couldn't see herself waiting in that dingy room for him to return. Knowing Stanley, it might be hours.

From the bottom of the stairwell, she peered into the cavernous tavern in the back of the Dixie.

The neon beer signs above the wall-length mirror behind the bar outlined the shadowy shapes of women with puffed up hair. Prostitutes!

Denise spotted an empty booth against the wall and sat facing the door. No one came for a drink order, so she held up a finger. When the bartender looked her way, he kept polishing glasses like he couldn't see her. After waving at the bartender without results, she edged between two barstools and placed an order for a double Chivas on the rocks.

The gorilla looked at her like she was from outer space. "Johnny Walker's the best I can do."

Denise flicked at him with the back of her hand,

but he didn't move. He apparently wanted a verbal response before he poured.

"Yes, of course. That'll be fine."

"Like your style, Hon," remarked the woman on her right.

Denise wanted to go back to the booth to wait for her drink, but the woman swiveled her stool and continued to talk.

"Shows you got some class. Class always sells, I say."

"Sell? No ..." Denise didn't know what to say next that the woman might not take as an offence. The last thing she needed was a catfight with a pissed-off whore. She felt so humiliated, tears formed in her eyes.

"Now, now, dear ..." The woman put her hand on Denise's shoulder. "I didn't mean to scare you. I ain't seen you in here before is all and wanted you to know somebody in this place is friendly."

She spoke louder now; her voice aimed at the bartender whose back was turned stretching to a shelf above the mirror for a bottle. "Old sourpuss back there, runs half the women off that come in here." The bartender grinned over his shoulder. "Don't pay him no-never-mind. He figures he gets paid to act mean, but he's a pussycat really, if you get to know him." The woman winked, "And I reckon I know him."

The barkeep came back with the bottle, glass full of ice and a crafty smile. "She's right. You ain't got nothing to worry about in this place. It's just we don't get many girls coming in dressed to the nine's like you and asking for liquor off the top shelf."

These two beamed welcoming smiles and Denise

couldn't help but smile back. A person can't have too many friends, she thought, even among the lower classes, "I was just passing by and needed a drink." She drained half the glass. "I've had a hard day."

The hooker stared at the wedding ring Denise still wore. "Man trouble? Ain't getting what you need at home, I'm betting."

Denise couldn't hold it back any longer. She tried to hide her face but tears dribbled through her fingers.

"Tucker, get your ass on down the bar and clean some glasses or something. Let us women talk."

Denise kept her hands covering her face, her shoulders heaving. Purple mascara leaked down to her chin. The prostitute poked at the back of her hands with a wad of bar napkins.

"I'm not a whore."

The prostitute chuckled, leaning in close to see Denise's eyes between her fingers.

"Now, now, Hon. You shouldn't think of it that way. All women are whores, you know. Me, I've known I was a whore since twelve years old."

"I was ..." Denise pulled her hand away from her face to display the diamond, "I'm married."

"And your husband is going to meet you here, is that right?"

Denise withdrew her hand back to her face to sob some more. The prostitute's hand pressed against her arm. Denise was afraid this floozy might try to hug her.

"Hon, every girl that comes in here is a whore. Some have wedding rings, like you. I've been married a few times myself, but even then, I was a whore. It's just a word, like that ring is just a ring. Put it in

your purse and you can be who you want to be."

Denise slapped her hands on the counter defiantly. "You don't understand. I'm here to find ... my lover. He was supposed to meet me. We're madly in love, you see. We're going to be married just as soon ..." Denise caught herself beginning to babble, justifying herself to this whore, and then went on anyway. "I've got to see him tonight. It's been too long. I need him to ..."

The prostitute returned a knowing smile. "It's OK, Hon. What you need is a good fucking. That always clears things up for me."

Denise stared back slack-faced and then finished her drink. There was no point arguing the point.

"You got anything in that purse to tidy up with? If he's coming, you want to look your best. If he's gotten tied up somewhere else—boys will be boys, you know—there will be other guys in later who will be glad to fill the bill. The restrooms are at the end of the bar."

When Denise exited the restroom, she was startled to see the prostitute standing away from the bar with her arm draped around Stanley's shoulder. Denise slid into the first dimly lit booth she came to.

Stanley nodded his head and smiled before going back to the stairwell in the lobby. The prostitute returned to the bar to sit with another of the whores. She patted the other woman's arm and then moved down the bar to talk with the bartender.

Denise wanted to follow Stanley upstairs, burst in, and surprise him. She imagined his startle. But then would he wave her to the bed or erupt in anger? What if he didn't want her anymore? He might not even try to lie; just throw her out. Her heart ached, physically ached. The suspicion that had nagged at her all week resurfaced. He could have met her at Armand's if he'd wanted. He was up there waiting for one of these whores. He'd moved on, forgotten about her.

The prostitute sitting alone at the bar gulped her drink and headed for the front door. She stood for a moment between the doorway and the stairwell as if making a decision, and then went upstairs.

At home, Denise tried to sleep, cried, took pills. The thought of that whore in Stanley's bed kept coming back. She cried some more, got a fresh pillow, took more pills, thought of ways to lure Stanley back—or if that failed, get even. By morning light, she had finally dozed off; then Nina knocked and came in with a tray of pastries. Denise shooed her out so vehemently, Nina splashed coffee onto the croissants while setting the tray on the dressing table.

Denise rushed to the bathroom and gagged over the commode. If she could throw up, she might feel better. She sloshed cold water in her face, then stood back looking into the mirror. Her cheeks were baggy and sallow. Crow's feet radiated from the corners of her eyes. The woman in the mirror looked old, worn out.

Her lips pressed tight into a line; her eyes became steely. She had to go back, get this over with. She'd claw his eyes out.

She drove first to the café on Charlotte where he got his breakfast. She ordered coffee and waited. The waitress and the customers kept glancing at her like she had been beamed onto the wrong planet. Seething anger was topped off with humiliation. She left a twenty on the table and stalked out, marching with long strides toward the Dixie.

There was no hesitation now. Her brain was too tired to think. There was no plan other than to confront Stanley, blow up in his face. She used her key and flung the door wide.

A woman's bare ass glared at her from the window. That whore from last night teetered over the windowsill; her dress pulled up above her waist and her rump stuck up like a bitch in heat. Denise kicked the mocking eye in the center as hard as she could with the toe of her stiletto.

* * *

As Rachael finished reading, a pop came from the street below and then two more. *Gunshots!* She rushed to the window.

Chapter 42

Detective Duffy stepped on the perp's wrist and bent down to ease the revolver from his fingers. He'd just blown two dime-size holes through the guy's chest, but he felt for a pulse at his neck anyway. Wide-eyed shock, a last thought, was frozen on the man's face. The pupils of his eyeballs continued to expand and contract independently for a second, until they too were stilled by death. Duffy formed the index and pinky fingers of his right hand into a Texas Longhorn salute and closed the eyes.

Above the ringing in his ears from the 9MM blasts, came a yelp like from a stepped-on Chihuahua; then a thud. Duffy jerked to his feet, both guns out front at arm's length. Light-headed vertigo caused a soft-shoe dance as he panned down the sights of the Glock. The scene dimmed. Gold flakes drifted across his vision. He reminded himself to breathe. He stopped rigid when he saw the second crumpled body. Behind the body, a woman's head popped up from behind a parked car and then ducked with a shriek when he aimed at her.

Time stuttered to a stop. His skin tingled, muscles coiled to react to what might come next. Only the guns trembling in front of him moved. A second later—or maybe a minute—his body began to deflate like from a pinhole in a beach toy and his arms lowered slowly. The rest of the world crept back into focus. He slipped the revolver into his pocket and fumbled the Glock back into its shoulder holster.

A skinny man rushed out of the Dixie Hotel entrance and stumbled into the woman sprawled on the sidewalk. The palms of his hands flew out to fend off the horror as he walked backward into the lobby. Duffy continued to watch through the plate glass front as the man circled behind a counter and punched three numbers into the desk phone. The man fished a pack of cigarettes from the pocket of his Hawaiian shirt, but then threw the pack on the counter and jabbed his index finger toward the street as he yelled into the receiver. Good, Duffy thought, backup's on the way.

He should check the woman; see if she was still alive. It would just be a procedural formality. From twenty yards, he could see her skull was crushed. Blood from ears and mouth fed a rapidly spreading pool under her head. Her heart might still be beating, but she would bleed out before an ambulance arrived.

The adrenaline jitters began. Duffy backed up to a car parked at the curb and slid down to sit on the asphalt, clenching his arms around his knees to stop the shaking. Might as well just wait for the squad cars. He would be useless anyway until his heart rate subsided.

Duffy's eyes flicked around the scene, but his mind didn't register anything. He was thinking about his wife and the life insurance. What would have been the lump sum payout if the guy had been a better shot? What was a dead detective worth these days? How much would they dock his retirement check if he quit tomorrow? He was trying to remember the formula based on years of service.

The blare of sirens crept closer. The upper floor windows of the Dixie filled with faces—men pointing, women covering their mouths. The open window she had fallen from was empty except for the frilly curtains pushed outside rippling in the breeze.

Behind the glass front of the Dixie's lobby, a man stuffing his shirttail in his pants descended the stairway, eager to get away before a dragnet began. His woman friend, shoes in hands, sheepishly tiptoed behind him. Duffy knew he should secure the site, keep everybody inside. His heart pounded in his ears. He just couldn't make himself get up.

A classy blonde dashed out without even glancing at the body on the sidewalk. Her ombre-tinted hair hiding her downturned face would make a Vogue model envious. The debutante shuffle in conservative suit with matching heels set her apart from the prostitutes with smeared makeup and mussed hair bolting past her. He watched her scurry to the corner where she hailed a cab.

"Detective Duffy, are you hurt?" Burt Watkins, cub reporter for the Morning Gazette, ran toward him. With his police scanner, he almost always beat the squad cars to the scene.

"Naw, not really. Hey Burt, see if you can get the number off that cab ... ?" But as he pointed, the cab pulled away. "Never mind."

Watkins rushed from one body to the other taking pictures with his little digital camera. His thick auburn hair reflected orange highlights from the sun like the coat of an Irish setter. He reminded Duffy of the son he'd never had.

When Burt returned, Duffy had gotten to his feet, but still leaned on the car.

"Detective, what's going on?"

"Dammit Burt. Give me a minute, will you? Let the boys get the crime scene tape up. After the lab folks get things under control, after the pictures; then we'll talk. You were first on the scene, so I'll give you an exclusive."

"Did you know either of them?"

"Not really. This guy was a suspect I was trailing when he pulled a gun."

"What about the girl, know her? She one of the known hookers?"

"Haven't seen her up close yet."

Burt manipulated his camera until pictures flashed onto the tiny screen. He clicked through the images until he found a close-up. Duffy glanced at it and then grabbed the camera out of Bert's hand for a closer look. Another shot of adrenaline surged through his body. He weaved a little as he plodded over to confirm it was her.

Holding his badge out front, Duffy elbowed through a circle of gawkers. "Back up folks. If you saw any of this, give your name and where you can be reached to Officer Roberts here." He taps the patrolman guarding the body on the shoulder. "Unless you're a witness, you need to leave."

A man on his knees beside her, intent on examining every inch of exposed flesh, didn't move. The putrid smell of dried sweat and street grime encrusted on the man's overcoat made Duffy's stomach lurch. Yellowish strands of hair that looked like it had never been cut dangled onto her bare stomach. Duffy's fingers clutched into fists as he fought the impulse to beat the guy to a pulp.

"You too, buddy." Duffy lifted him roughly by the elbow and shoved him toward the uniformed policeman.

She'd landed on the crown of her head and then flopped to her back. At first, he thought the hair a few feet away was hers before he recognized it as a wig. The skull was flattened, face distorted, but it was her all right—the psychiatrist, Dr. Henley. "Damn! Damn, damn, damn—"

"Can I quote you on that?" Burt had followed him.

Duffy removed his jacket, inched to the edge of the blood pool, and covered her head. The tan fabric took on a pink tinge as the blood wicked into it.

"Burt, give me your jacket."

Burt didn't move.

"Come on, off with it. If the cleaners can't get the stains out, you can turn it in on your expense report."

Duffy covered her pubic area. She was even bloody there.

Squad cars, sirens blasting, arrived from both ends of the street almost at the same time. Duffy met briefly with a sergeant before the uncoiling of the yellow barrier tape began. The patrolmen from the other car headed into the Dixie entrance. The different siren tone of ambulances approached. Another squad car squealed to a halt. Men in blue pushed aside curious bystanders as the ambulances backed up to the victims.

Twenty minutes later, Duffy waved Burt over to his car. They got in and rolled up the windows even though it was already sultry.

"Put that recorder away. What I'm about to tell you is off the record until the next-of-kin are notified. If I see any quotes I didn't authorize in tomorrow's paper, I'll have a talk with your editor. Understand?"

"Sure, sure. I know the routine."

"The guy's name is Fred Troster. I've never had a run-in with him before, but he has been questioned at the station a few times—that Foster blackmail case last winter, a couple of robberies before that. Slick. We never could gather enough evidence to book him on anything.

"Her name is Dr. Rachel Henley, a psychiatrist at Virgin Mother Hospital. I've worked with her ... " Duffy watched as the attendants loaded her shrouded body into an ambulance, "on homicide investigations. And no, she's not a hooker on the side. And no, I have no idea why she's lying dead on the sidewalk."

"Give me more."

"Back off, Burt. I've got unsolved homicides coming out my ass right now. I'll tell you what I know are facts, to give you a head start. Beyond that, you're on your own." A smile crept onto Duffy's face looking at the alert young go-getter, Irish setter hair, should-have-been son. "Mister hot-shot reporter."

Duffy wanted to help him out, but any speculation would get them both in trouble. What did he have, anyway? Counting the two added today—four bodies. Murders? Probably. Related to each other? Maybe. Lots of suspicions; all conjecture based on a whodunit written by one of the dead bodies. None of it added up to anything he could call evidence.

It was going to be a long summer. Again, he savored the thought of quitting tomorrow; taking the wife on one of those Caribbean cruises she'd talked about. Duffy scrunched down in the driver's seat and looked at nothing through the windshield. The adrenaline had worn off, leaving his body craving sleep.

"Burt … ? Burt, have you ever heard of a Muse?"

There was no response. When Duffy looked over, Burt's perplexed, yet wary expression brought back his smile.

"I'm serious. Tell me everything you know about Muses."

"This is a little out of context, don't you think, considering we've got two bodies on the way to the morgue right now."

"Humor me, Burt. Show off that college education your daddy paid for. Off the record, just you and me."

"In Greek mythology, there are nine Muses, all daughters of Zeus. As the story goes, they're the source of all inspiration. If you intuitively think of something, supposedly it's because of the Muses. They cause things to happen by inspiring people."

Duffy sat up straight. "Say it again—the last part."

"A Muse causes things to happen by inspiring people."

"Are they real, Burt?"

Burt's head slowly panned around to glare at Duffy with a *you're-an-idiot* expression.

"I mean in the same way electricity is real. In that tape recorder of yours, do you really believe little negative signs are shooting through the wires at the speed of light? We know electricity is real because of what it does. But what is it exactly? Could a Muse be like that, Burt, a placeholder for some magic we'll never understand?"

Catalpa Trees

Gramps says bamboo fishing poles alone is ample proof, but to further reveal his true nature, God made the catalpa tree for growing fishing worms. He told me a catalpa tree was right there beside the apple tree in the Garden of Eden. Things would be a whole lot different if Adam had got to that catalpa tree first and gone fishing like God intended, instead of listening to Eve about that apple.

Mister Shumpert, the farm next over from Gramps, is blessed with two giant catalpa trees in his backyard. That's where me and Gramps headed on the morning of Confederate Memorial Day. Each of us carried a long tapered pole over our shoulders and a five-gallon lard stand in our off hands. Gramps' bucket was still a quarter-full. He had in mind catching a mess of bream and then frying 'em up over an open fire before the rest of the crowd got there. My bucket was empty; that's where we was gonna put the worms.

Catalpa trees are purty in the spring when they're a bloom. But over in the middle of the summer, they get raggedy. The worms eat half of each leaf—not half the leaves, but half of each leaf. The veins in the leaves must be tough, so they leave that part sticking up like the skeleton of a hand. And then there are the purple and green seedpods—Gramps calls 'em Indian cigars—that dangle from the tips of the limbs. By Halloween, them seedpods have split open and dangle from the twisted limbs like gnarly fingers. Them trees look spooky even in the daytime.

Gramps boosted me up to the crotch of the first limb, and I shinnied on my belly out along the limb till I got to the worms.

They're little fuzzy caterpillars about an inch long, black with yellow stripes, and a shiny knob on one end for a head. There were millions of 'em. If I tried to pick one off a leaf, it curled up and fell to the ground, so when I found one, I'd pluck off the whole leaf and drop it. Gramps caught the leaf in the empty lard bucket. It wasn't long before we were off through the pasture toward Berg's Lake.

"If'n we catch one fish for every two worms, we can feed the whole camp, I figure," Gramps said. The bream were still on-bed the day before when my buddy Mickey and me was down there, so I speculated we'd catch all we wanted. I started to run ahead, but Gramps called me back.

"You ain't gettin' no head start. We'll throw in at the same time and we'll see if'n I don't catch more. The Coon-on-a-Log won't start 'til after noon, so we'll have two or three hours to catch a mess before we start a fire."

Berg's Lake is the campground for the community. The Baptist men built a bunch of picnic tables under the trees and they hold services there in the hot summer. It's convenient for the baptizing. And the Pentecostals have revivals there. Me and Mickey snuck off down there one night in the fall to watch. Mickey said they speak in tongues, roll around on the ground, and handle snakes and such. They'd stirred up a cloud of dust around their bonfire, but Mickey chickened out and wouldn't get close enough to see them handling the snakes.

The big event for the year is the Coon-on-a-Log held on Confederate Memorial Day, the last Monday in April. All the denominations turn out for that. That's like the World Series for coon dogs. All the coon hunters save up the coons they'd caught during the winter. When they knocked a coon from a tree, they beat back the dogs to keep it alive. Mister Riley kept four or five in cages behind his blacksmith shed that he'd be abringin'. It was gonna be a sight.

"Dad-burn, Bud! Did you bring a stringer? How we gonna keep them fish fresh if we ain't got no stringer? Run on back to the house and get some twine—or some balin' wire will do. You can be to the barn and back before I even get to the lake."

I took off at a run before I got suspicious and pulled up. "Now don't you start fishin' 'fore I get back."

"All right, I won't. I'll wait right here if'n you don't trust me. Just get on now."

When I got to the barn, I found a couple of wires that had been clipped off hay bales that would work fine. I was about to run back when I took notice of the apple trees beside the path from the barn to the house. The apples were still green, but they'd sure taste good sliced and fried up with the fish, so I started picking some into a feed sack.

As I worked my way toward the house, I heard the screen door slam and Granny come out the back door carrying the enamel pot she keeps on the back of the cook stove. That same pot has been on the back of the stove as long as I remember. She uses the hot water for washing dishes, or scalding the skins off tamaters, and such.

The way she struggled, both hands on the bail to keep it from sloshing, it musta been full. She carried it to her flowerbed beside the garden and slowly poured it out. The steam rose in front of her as the water hit the ground.

I couldn't figure it. If she was watering her flowers, she wouldn't use hot water. If she was just getting rid of dirty dishwater, she wouldn't be pouring it in her flowerbed. Them flowers was her pride and joy. She stood there a minute staring at where she'd poured the water. I thought about running to the house to ask about it, but Gramps and fishing were waiting, so I throwed the apple sack on my shoulder and ran toward the lake.

We fished on the slough end of the lake where you could see the wallowed-out holes of the bream beds. Gramps fished in the beds where Mickey and me had already caught 'em all out. I knew exactly where the bream were, so I caught the most. It didn't take long till we had as many as we could fry.

On the way back to the tables, Gramps and me picked up sticks to start a fire. Mister Riley and his mule had pulled a downed tree to the lake and he was busy with his ax lopping off limbs and chopping the trunk into a six-foot length. There was plenty of wood chips to burn.

Mister Riley is a blacksmith by day and a coon hunter by night. He's a big-chested man with kinky hair tuftin' out'a his overalls like he's half wild. His dogs were tied off to trees on one side of the campground and the coons were in cages on the other side. The other hunters started arriving with their dogs and coons and helped Mister Riley get ready.

Mickey's daddy is the strongest man around 'cepting for Mister Riley, so they waited till he showed up to roll the log in the water. After the log quit spinning and found its floating side, Mister Riley nailed a big fence staple in the middle. This is where he'd clip the coon's chain. Mister Riley waded out chest deep and anchored the log with a rope tied to a rock.

Granny walked up carrying a pail containing the rest of the fixings. Buster pranced alongside like he was escorting royalty. Buster's a collie with four white feet and a blaze on his forehead; right handsome compared to them coon dogs that look like they been sleeping in a pig wallow. Buster sat on his rump with perfect manners watching all the goings-on, like it was all being put on for his benefit. That collie wouldn't have nothing to do with those coon dogs. He wouldn't even sniff tails with 'em. Granny said Buster don't want nobody thinking he's any kin to them dumb coon dogs.

Granny's pail contained the meal, and an onion, and buttermilk. She diced the onion and stirred it into the meal and buttermilk she'd mixed in her pail. She brought an extra Mason jar of cool buttermilk for me and Gramps to sip on while we built up the fire. When the fire burned down, Gramps pushed up some rocks around the coals and set his lard stand on 'em.

Me and Gramps gutted and scaled the bream with our pocketknives. We counted out thirty big ones before washing off the slime in the lake. Gramps dumped 'em, one at a time, into the hushpuppy batter before slipping 'em into the bubbling lard. They jumped around like they'd come back to life.

After the fish were cooked, Granny took over with the hush puppies. A spoonful of dough turned into a brown ball. I was at her elbow begging her to dip one out for me to taste. She said that turning brown don't mean they ain't raw in the middle. She couldn't explain how she knowed when they were done, but said it'd be one of those things I'd just know when I got older. I sliced up the apples and she throwed 'em in there too. She wiped down one of the picnic tables with her apron and laid out the food in rows on a red-checkered oilcloth. She threw the hem of the cloth over the food to keep the flies off until time to eat.

By the time we finished cooking, the place had crowded up. The women laid out what food they brung while the men inspected the coons. They spit tobacco juice in their faces to see which had the most fight. Kids and dogs were running everywhere. Granny stood guard over the food with a willow switch. After Reverend Barker prayed for the souls of Confederate soldiers and blessed the food, we ate. Everything was ready for the show.

Mister Riley, wearing a leather shirt now and welder's gloves, drug the cage of the first coon to the water's edge. The coon bowed up and hissed like a tomcat. He convinced me to stand back. Mister Riley reached into the cage and held the coon's head down while he snapped a three-foot length of well chain onto its collar. It was the bravest thing I ever saw. He waded out to the log, pulling the coon thrashing in the water behind him. After clipping the chain to the log, the coon swam around trying to get away and eventually pulled itself up onto the log.

When the dogs heard the coon hissing, the whole bunch of 'em barked and lunged at their chains. You never heard such a racket. Each hunter picked one dog out'a his pack and held it by the collar at the water's edge until all the dogs were ready. Mister Riley gave the signal and then it was the hunters' turn to do the hollering. Each hunter had his own special hoot or whistle to rile his dogs to a frenzy. When the dogs still chained to trees heard those calls, they half strangled themselves to get in the action. Buster sat beside Granny and seemed only slightly mused by it all.

Some coons didn't last no time. They got snatched off'n the log by the first dog that swam out. Other times the dogs paddled round and round the log until they gave out and, one at a time, headed back. When one of them dogs made it to shore, the owner snatched it up roughly by the collar, kicked it in the ribs, and drug it back to its chain. The other hunters laughed and pointed saying the dog wasn't worth the bullet to shoot it. But even if the coon won the first round, the hunters readied a fresh pack of dogs. Eventually, a dog got brave enough to grab the coon by the leg and while the coon was biting that dog, it would get dumped into the water and be finished off by the rest of the dogs. When the dogs swam back in, their snouts were dripping blood from the scratches and bites, but they didn't seem to mind.

I told Gramps this didn't seem like no fair contest.

Gramps explained, "bein' as a coon dog is the dumbest creature God ever created, and coons are nigh on the smartest, you had to use more'n one dog at a time to equal things out. And besides, this ain't about the coons at all. It's a contest 'tween the hunters to see who raised up the bravest dogs. And don't be feeling sorry for the coons, neither. Them coons would'a been cooked for supper months ago if'n it weren't for the hunters savin' 'em." Looking down at my snarl, Gramps patted my head. "It'll all make sense when you get growed up—when you look at it like a man does."

Mister Riley saved his best dog and the best coon for last. The big boar coon was half again bigger than the other coons and blacker and meaner looking. His ears were tattered and one eye milky. He was as big as the dogs.

Gramps told me, "Riley caught Bear hisself, but not 'fore he kilt his best dog. And that weren't Bear's first tussle neither. Every coon hunter inside twenty miles knows that coon and respectfully refers to him as Bear. Bear probably kills more dogs every year than Mister Riley kills coons."

Mister Riley let out a yelp when he snapped the chain to Bear's collar. Bear was drug out of the cage with his bared teeth snarling at the crowd. Gramps lifted me up on a picnic table and stood in front of Granny in case he got a-loose. A dust cloud rose as he clawed the ground pulling against the chain. We was all relieved when Mister Riley finally drug him in the water and hooked him to the log. Upon reaching shore again, Mister Riley slung off the leather glove and blood poured out. Bear had got him good.

The dogs rounded the log several times, snapping at Bear's legs, and got their noses sliced open by sharp claws for their effort. The dogs started back to shore—all but Mister Riley's dog. He didn't have the energy to lunge at Bear no more, but he wasn't giving up. Bear jumped on the dog's head and clamped onto his snout with his teeth before they both went underwater. The water swirled a time or two before Bear popped up and climbed back onto the log. The dog floated up later.

Granny was wrapping Mister Riley's hand in a lard-soaked rag while he watched. When the hind end of his dog drifted to the surface, he jerked his hand away and rushed to the shore. I thought he was going to swim out to that log hisself. I believe he thought about it. Instead, he turned back to the crowd, tilted his head to the sky, and commenced to curse. The reverend was sitting right in front of him and there were women-folk all around, but he let out some awful words like he was by hisself out in a cornfield and chopped his toe with a hoe. He ran back through the crowd to the tree where his dogs were tethered and let them all loose. He shooed 'em into the water and sloshed in up to his knees to urge 'em on. Those dogs had been out before and were tired but still eager. As they dog-paddled around the log, Bear reached out and pushed their heads underwater until they was all drowned. Mister Riley, his mouth hanging open, his hand dripping blood in the water, watched the awful sight.

That's where he remained, him and Bear staring at each other across the water while everybody else quietly packed up to leave. Granny and Buster went to home, but I stayed with Gramps to see how things turned out. Gramps said if the hate passing between them two was turned into fire, the whole lake would be aboil.

The sun was headed down when Mister Riley picked up his ax and waded out toward the log. Bear stretched the chain to the far end of the log. Mister Riley arched back the ax and come down with all his might. The ax whacked through the chain and buried into the log. He left Bear and the ax teetering on the log and waded to shore. He didn't seem to be in a talking mood, so we didn't say nothing. He gathered up all his dog chains, mounted his mule, and galloped up the trail beside the lake.

Gramps said he figured them two would meet again. It would take Riley two years to raise up a new pack of hounds, but if Bear was still alive, Riley'd be after him. "Sometimes a man's just got to square things up and start over," he said. "You'll understand one day."

It was dusk when we got back to the barn. An oil lamp lit up the kitchen window. While I put up the poles in the barn, Gramps went on to the house. When I got there, he was over at the flowerbed on his knees, the same place Granny poured the water.

Before Granny went off to bed, she'd left white beans and cold chicken on the kitchen table and a pone of cornbread warming on the stovetop. We would need buttermilk, so I got the jug from the icebox and some jelly glasses before I sat down. Gramps came in with a hangdog look.

"Bud, I figure it's a sign. The good Lord must'a caught me a-sinnin'." Gramps plopped in the chair across the table. "The first time I planted them catalpa cuttin's out by the smokehouse, I figure it was the salt leachin' into the soil what kilt 'em. Then when I planted some more in the orchard and they died off, I thought the rotten apples had soured the soil. So last full moon, I got some volunteers from under Shumpert's trees and transplanted 'em to the flowerbed.

"Lee said she wasn't abiding it; said catalpa trees was too ugly to have around the house. And if'n they took hold and grew, them worms would turn into sphinx moths that would flap every night at the screen door and slip in the house with the comings-and-goings and wind up in her cook pots, the churn, and everywhere.

"I told Lee that it's every man's birthright to have a worm tree in his yard. It's all but promised in the Bible. I had to be the man of the house and put my foot down. You'll see, when you get growed. Men make the decisions and women-folk just got to live with it. That's in the Bible, too."

A solitary moth fluttered around the globe of the lamp in the center of the table sending shadows crawling around the walls. Gramps reached out and swatted it like it was a demon sent to taunt him.

"Now them shoots I planted in the flowerbeds done shriveled up. That's the best soil on the property. There ain't no reason cept'n it's a sign that I ain't gonna be allowed no fishin' worm trees. His ways is mysterious, but I reckon I'll heed His judgment.

"Will I understand when I get older, Gramps?"

Gramps took a swig of buttermilk and studied the white beans he had smashed on his plate with a fork. "Reckon not, Bud. Some things a man's just gotta accept without knowin' the why of it."

The Widow's Tale

"Mother, you need to take a break. You'll make yourself sick staying here. He might be like this for weeks. Go home and sleep in a real bed. Come back tomorrow. A nurse will give you a call if there's any change."

When Simon says change, he means *death*. The only possible change would be for his father to die. Even though George's eyes are half-open and occasionally blink, Simon doesn't believe he is still conscious. Lucille, however, knows he can hear them. She can feel his presence.

"I'll stay," she says. "Come back after work, and I'll go home then."

Simon wipes a frost-colored curl from her forehead to make room for his kiss. He looks over at his father's expressionless face. He would usually pat his father's hand and speak to him before he left. But after watching his father's shallow breathing for a moment, he turns to the door. "I'll see you about six, then," he says as the door closes.

Lucille reaches under the cotton blanket and pulls out a pale hand that she presses to her lips. She feels for a pulse at his wrist although the monitor above the bed shows his heart is still weakly pumping. She holds the hand to her cheek and looks down into the dark pupils barely visible between his eyelids.

"Can you hear me?" she asks. "Blink if you can hear me."

Several seconds pass before his eyes flutter. She really doesn't need this response to know.

"There's no change to your condition, George. I didn't know if you picked that up from the doctor's visit this morning. He told me in the hall afterward that you may hang on for a few more days, but it would be a miracle if you lasted longer." She rubbed her cheek against the flaccid hand. "I really don't want a miracle. Do you George?"

She tucks the hand back under the blanket and walks to the single window that looks out on the street several stories below. Simon is just pulling into traffic. She goes into the tiny bathroom leaving the door open and runs cold water into a hand towel. After she brings it out in a wad, she unfurls it in front of his face. "Would you rather go now, George?" She holds it before him waiting for a response. His eyelids flutter again. The heartbeats on the monitor come closer together.

"Don't be afraid, George. I know you believe. God has forgiven your sins. You could be in heaven in just a few minutes. It would be over for you." Her face hovers above him with a compassionate smile. "And since you didn't do it to yourself, there'd be no sin."

She folds the towel several times, to the size of a notebook page, and displays it on her palm in front of his face before tenderly wiping a gleam of moisture from his forehead and cheeks.

"Of course, I would have to go to hell, wouldn't I, George? Nobody would suspect, but God would know, wouldn't He?"

A nurse comes in with a cheerful greeting. Lucille leaves the wet towel on George's forehead while the nurse checks the I V and records his vital signs before scurrying out to finish her rounds.

"You've preached from your pulpit on Sundays about mortal sins, willful sins—how there's no absolution. You think this will send me to Hell, don't you, George? But it won't. What I'm doing for you won't matter to God."

Lucille scoots a straight-backed chair closer to the bed and sits down. Her bleary eyes focus on her hands folded on her lap.

"Do you remember when I first told you I was pregnant with Simon, back when you had your first church over in Wren? Oh, we were so happy then. Everything was happening so fast for us. You named him Simon, after your father, that very night. You knew it would be the boy you'd prayed for.

"You told the church elders the next day. And the day after that, I took a bus to see Momma. It was then I discovered it wasn't true. I stayed an extra day with Momma because I couldn't think how to tell you. That night, on my way back to you, I got raped in some deserted town where I waited to change buses. You remember what I looked like when I finally got home, how I couldn't stop crying? I told you everything. Everything, except about me not being pregnant.

"We didn't have a car. Even if we could get back to the town, you said the guy would be gone by then anyway. If we reported it, things might get turned around somehow and look bad for your career. You started talking like it was my fault for being so stupid. You couldn't figure out what to do and soon it was too late to do anything.

"Then I found I really was pregnant. And everybody at the church was so nice to us—the shower and all. Simon came, and he was so beautiful. You thought he looked just like you.

"For me, the rape was becoming a distant memory, but it kept eating at you, George. You said you couldn't touch me without thinking about it, about him, the unknown man who had defiled me, with whom I had fornicated. We haven't slept together in twenty years, George. Did you realize it had been that long?

"I still dream about that rape every night and wake up in a sweat. Did you know that? I wish I could have talked to you about it—to anybody. But of course, I couldn't. After a few years, I began to forget the man's face so the dream didn't scare me as much." She again wipes his neck and forehead with the wet cloth. "But the face came back, George. It's Simon's face."

She leans forward searching the eyes that seem to be focused on her. Drops of moisture had collected in the corners.

"Please don't hate me, George. Hate is a sin that would keep you from your reward. You might wind up in hell with me forever. That would be like double hell, wouldn't it?"

She wipes the tears from his eyes and leaves the cloth spread over his face below his eyes.

"What I'm doing for you is just an additional mortal sin for me, don't you see? After the sin of having sex with another man, and the sin of not telling you about Simon, it doesn't matter. My soul's going to hell anyway. You understand, don't you, George?"

Buster

Granny ain't mean enough to make me mind. Momma's not neither—normally. But if she's in one of her moods, she'll go to the closet and pull out a wire coat hanger. She stretches it out, like the shaft of a flyswatter, and forms the hook into a handle. My choices then are to run or back down. Of course, I try running first. There's no way she can catch me. I can't help but laugh when she tries, but that makes things worse. She gets that look and just leaves the hanger on the dinner table till I come back. I gotta eat sometime, she figures. She won't go softhearted 'bout it neither; no use begging at that point, not after she's bent the hanger. So I take the beating plus do, or not do, what she says.

Momma's on some trip to Birmingham with her doctor to get her rash checked out. It flares up in the summer, and she has to go to Birmingham or Memphis with the doctor to get some tests done. So I'm staying at Granny's till she gets back.

Granny and Gramps live on a farm the next county over from where me and Momma live. I like staying here. I get to do pretty much whatever suits me. And they've got pigs and chickens and a milk cow I can chase or chunk rocks at. They're gonna get rid of the milk cow 'cause Gramps can't milk no more on account of his being sick, and Granny's scared of the cow, and Uncle Leon won't do it.

Uncle Leon lives here too. He's Momma's youngest brother. He sleeps in the back bedroom, the one Gramps ain't in. Gramps calls it "the kids' room." The kids' room has two big beds. Momma says one bed was for the boys and the other for the girls when she was growing up. When Leon came along, Gramps walled in half the back-porch 'cause there weren't no more room in the boys' bed. But since all the other kids got married and moved out, Leon sleeps in the girls' bed now, the softer of the two. When I'm there, I take the little bed on the sleeping porch he used to sleep in. Leon don't like me in the same room as him, and I don't like it neither. Plus it's cooler on the porch in the summertime.

Leon's my only problem here. He wants to be my boss all the time. Whenever Granny can't get me to do something, she brings in Leon. Gramps used to make me do stuff, but he's in bed all the time, so Granny gets Leon to do it.

Like this business of washing my face; I get these blackheads and sometimes they fester up into whiteheads. Granny says it's 'cause I won't wash my face. I don't argue with her. She's little, not much taller than me, sort of a wrinkled bag of skin, like a coin purse, so I don't argue none with her, just give her a "yessum" and forget about it.

So, when Leon came in yesterday—he works in town at some office—she told him. He made me sit at the kitchen table. With Granny standing behind him, he explained about pimples and how they'd scar up my face like Uncle Russ's. But I guess he could tell he wasn't getting nowhere and was going to be late picking up some girl, so he finally quit with the talking and grabbed my arm and drug me to the bathroom. The bathroom is right there between the kitchen and the sleeping porch. Gramps put in the indoors bathroom when he walled in the back porch for Leon.

I thought he was going to whip me, but he told me real stern-like to wash my face and closed the door. When I opened the door, Leon was still there and saw my face was wet from splashing the water, but he slammed the door and yelled for me to do it with soap or he'd do it himself. Him being late for his date and all, I figured he might and be rough about it too. When I came out the next time, he marched me over to Granny for inspection.

"Do it every day before I get home," he warned. "Or I'll hold you down and do it with a scrub brush."

Leon's mean that way. It's not like he wasn't the baby of the family and didn't get away with stuff himself. He's put Granny through the wringer, Momma says. After Leon left, I went straight out to the garden behind the house and threw dirt up in the air and let it rain down on me. Granny watched from the kitchen window. I guess I wanted her to see. She didn't yell or nothing, but she'd probably tell Leon.

I looked around for Buster, Leon's collie dog that was usually right beside me when he heard the screen door slam. He would have enjoyed the dirt throwing. I whistled for him, but he didn't come.

Buster and me were close like that. Whatever I did was okay with him. And I knew I could count on Buster. Sunday afternoon, a week ago, before Momma left, when the whole family was out under the water oak in the front yard receiving guests, I caught Leon on the back of the head with an acorn. He grabbed me up and started whipping me before I could get away. Momma was there and told him to quit, but she probably figured I deserved it, so she didn't get up. But Buster was after Leon in a second, growling and barking. Buster couldn't abide nobody getting whipped. While Leon was taking a swat at Buster, I wiggled free. Leon was beside himself, mad at both of us, but he couldn't catch neither one of us running. He did get a good kick in on Buster that caused him to yelp. Buster ran off, but I stayed and pestered Leon any way I could.

After Buster didn't come for the dirt throwing, I looked for him until dark. He didn't come in that night for the table scraps Granny threw out neither.

The next morning, I found him in a wallow he'd made under a hydrangea bush bordering the front porch. He was sprawled out on his stomach, but he wasn't napping like I first thought. His head was up, and his eyes seemed to be smiling, but he didn't get to his feet. He was panting, even though it wasn't hot yet. Houseflies swarmed around him. There was a funny, sweet smell.

I ran to the kitchen for Granny 'cause I knew something was wrong. She followed me back through the side yard, with me urging her to hurry up.

Buster struggled onto his front legs but couldn't get balanced on his hind legs, and finally settled back on his stomach. Granny studied him, first standing over him and then kneeling down. She fingered a greasy spot on his back. When Granny pulled the hair aside, a hole the size of a quarter stared back at us. You could look right into his body at a wiggling pulp inside.

Granny left me rubbing his head and came back with scissors and a hurricane lamp. She sheared the hair away from the hole in his back, then took the globe and metal part off the lamp and poured kerosene into the hole. Maggots started crawling out. She poured the kerosene in several times until she could better see down in the hole. The smell of the kerosene made me sick.

"Did somebody shoot him?" I asked.

"I reckon not," she said. "Looks like somethin's broke loose in his gut. Infection's eatin' at him from the inside made that hole."

She stood up and was thinking. I can't ever tell what Granny's thinking by looking at her 'cause of all the loose skin and wrinkles.

"Get him some water, Bud. Don't try to make him get up," she said finally.

When I got back with a bowl, Granny was gone. I could hear her voice quiet-like coming through the front bedroom window. The curtains were drawn, and I imagined her on the ladder-back chair by the head of the bed, discussing Buster with Gramps.

"Mister Wilkes wants to talk with you," she said when she came back out. She calls Gramps "Jerold" but wanted me to call him "Mister Wilkes."

I went in the front door into the parlor, and then through the open doorway to the front bedroom. The oily smell of coal from the fireplace mixed with the smell of Gramps. He still had hair, but it was completely white, and you could see through to his scalp. You could look through his face too, like it was made of candle wax, and see the blue veins underneath. He was propped up on two pillows. Granny must have helped him prop up like that for our talk.

"Go over to my closet, look in the back," he said. Closets flanked both sides of the fireplace. The one on the parlor side was Granny's and the one by the window was Gramps's. The doorframe had a wood block that you turned on a nail to open the door. It was dark inside, but you could see in if you opened the door wide to let in the light from the window. Overalls hung from nails on the sides, and a broom handle was suspended across the back of the closet, holding wire hangers for Gramps's church clothes.

"In the corner there's a rifle. See it?"

It was there. I could make out the shape of the stock underneath the hang-up clothes.

"Bring it over here."

I grabbed the cold barrel and brought it, holding it at arm's length, over to the bed.

"It ain't loaded, but don't go pointin' at me neither," Gramps said. He didn't reach for the gun, didn't seem to have the energy.

"Now listen up," he said. "Sit down there and listen to everything I say. I won't be saying it twice."

I sat in the chair next to the bed and put the butt of the gun on the floor and held the stock between my knees, both hands on the barrel. It was a little single-shot .22. The stock looked short enough for my arms. I wanted to throw it up and try it, but I waited.

"I was goin' to give this to you next Christmas, but you look big enough now. I traded Melvin Long outta it up at the courthouse. He used it for killin' hogs before he got lame. Now I'm goin' to tell you how it works, so listen good."

Without even lifting his head, he took me through how to open and close the chamber, how to cock it, and about the safety. He had me pull the trigger, and I jumped when the firing pin clicked.

"Now look in the dresser, top drawer toward the front. There's a box of bullets."

It was a full box of fifty with the bullets packed in neat rows. When I pulled a cartridge out, it gleamed like a new penny on my palm. He talked me through how to load a cartridge into the chamber.

"It won't fire yet 'cause you ain't cocked back the hammer. You don't do that till right before you shoot. Now open the chamber."

I operated the lever, moved the bolt back, and was surprised when the bullet popped out. I tried to catch the bullet before it hit the floor and almost dropped the gun.

"After you've fired, the empty shell case won't come out that easy. The chamber's worn. You might have to open the chamber a few times before it ejects an empty. If you still can't get the shell case out, you'll have to use your knife to pry it out. Whatever you do, don't use your knife to try to get a live bullet out, one that ain't been shot. If a live bullet gets stuck, come back and talk with me. Got it?"

I'd been thinking about the sound the bullet would make when I fired and maybe missed some of what he said, but I could figure it out. "Yessir," I said. "I think so."

Gramps craned his head around and stared at me. I could tell it took some effort. He wanted to see my face, to see if I was scared or not.

"You'll do all right," he said, trying to boost my confidence. "Take the rifle and the bullets down to the barn and do some practice shooting. Shoot 'em all up except for the last four or five. Put you a can up beside the barn and see if you can hit it. Don't be shooting back toward the house."

As I was leaving out the door, he strained to talk loud. "And make sure to take the bullet out before you come back to the house."

I was a natural with the gun. I hit the can every time after I got used to the sight. I thought about Buster hearing the gunshots, wanting to run, and not being able to. Buster was scared of guns. He was scared of fireworks too. Leon tied him to a tree to keep him from running off last Forth of July.

When I came marching back from the barn with the gun thrown on my shoulder, my hand under the butt like a soldier, Granny was at the kitchen window, watching.

"Is it loaded?" she wanted to know when I came in through the kitchen.

"Of course it ain't loaded," I said, forcing indignity into my voice. "You think I don't know to unload it?"

Granny would normally have slapped at me for my sass, but she didn't. She told me to go see Gramps. He wanted to know how the shooting went.

Gramps was still in bed; had been the entire week I'd been here. His eyes were closed, but the eyelids flicked up when I plopped in the chair. He squinted at first like it was too dark to make out who was there.

"Is it unloaded?" he asked.

"Yessir," I said.

"How'd you do?"

"Real good. I can hit anything," I blustered. "Sure is a sweet little gun."

"Rifle. Guns is what kids play with," he said. "I'll get Leon to pick you up some more shells tomorrow. Think you're ready for rabbits?"

"Yessir." I was squirming around on the seat just thinking about it.

"But first we need to do something." Gramps's face got serious like he was about to tell a secret. "We got to shoot Buster."

I stared back holding my breath trying to decide if I'd heard Gramps right. With the excitement of the rifle, I hadn't been thinking about Buster, and him laying just outside the window under the bush.

"What do you mean?"

"You know about Buster. You were the one what found him. Lee says he's sufferin'." Lee is what Gramps calls Granny. "Says he ain't gonna make it."

"He's got a sore on his back. It's just a sore. He'll be better in a couple of days."

"Lee knows these things. She says he needs shootin'."

Gramps was searching my face to see if I understood, and I was beginning to.

"Bud, Buster's fifteen. I 'member that 'cause I gave him to Leon on his fifth birthday, and now Leon's twenty. Fifteen's old for a dog."

"Well, you're old too, ain't ye? How'd you like somebody shooting you just 'cause you're old?"

"Yeah, I probably need shootin', too. But I ain't asking that."

Gramps and I stared at each other for a while. I was thinking about how I'd shoot Buster if I did it, whether in the heart or between the eyes. Then I started thinking about Gramps, where I'd shoot him.

"Make Leon do it," I said.

"He ain't tough enough on the insides. I reckon I know the boy well enough by now. And I can't make him do stuff no more. He'd talk his mother out of havin' to do it." Gramps's eyes closed slowly and I thought he'd dozed off. Then his eyes popped open. "Besides, them two grew up together. A man shouldn't have to shoot his own dog."

"Well, you can have your old gun back." I took it back to the closet and put it in the corner where I'd found it. When I came back to the bed, I didn't sit down. Gramps and I just looked at each other, figuring what to do next.

"Got any shells left?"

I dug in my pocket and pulled out five. I'd thrown the box away.

"Give 'em to Lee and tell her to come here." He didn't say it like he was mad, just resigned.

After doing what Gramps said, I went around and started swinging on the front porch swing. It screeched as I went back and forth. I could see Buster's legs under the bush. He hadn't moved at all. Through the open bedroom window, I could hear Gramps and Granny talking. I couldn't make out every word, but I heard my name and Buster's. I could also hear some words about the rifle. Gramps was going through the same thing with her that he had with me earlier.

When Granny came out the front door, she was holding the rifle by the barrel, out away from her like it was a snake she'd killed.

"Get on 'round back," she said to me.

I started to ask her what she was going to do, but I reckon I knew. She waited for me to get up, but I didn't.

"If you want to watch, then go ahead." Granny looked too tired to fight with me.

"I'll do it," I said. I got up and grabbed the rifle, but she didn't let go.

"You're too young. I told Jerold you're too young."

"I can do it. Now let me have that rifle before you shoot yourself."

She held on for a little while, looking back and forth between me and Buster's legs. When she let go of the rifle, she gave over the bullets with her other hand. She'd steeled herself to do it and sunk a little when she gave up the idea.

"Go on back in now. Ain't no sense in you watching," I told her. She opened the screen and I could hear the floorboards squeak on her way back to the kitchen. I couldn't see in the window, but I knew Gramps had been listening. I expected him to yell out something, but he didn't.

I sat back on the swing and loaded a bullet into the chamber. A roar started, like from a fire, like the house was burning down. Words crowded into my head. I knew I had to do it quick, right then, before the words started putting themselves together.

I walked around in front of the porch, in front of Buster. His head was still up, smiling and panting and watching me. He saw the rifle but didn't even try to get away. I put the end of the barrel on top of his head and closed my eyes before pulling the trigger.

I went to the shed and got a shovel and dug a hole in the orchard. I dug it shallow at first, just deep enough to cover him, and threw the shovel down. I wanted to get this over with, but I knew it wasn't deep enough. If Gramps had been there, he would have told me. So I picked up the shovel again and went another two feet deeper. I drug Buster by his hind legs from his wallow under the hydrangeas to beside the hole. He was too long, so I dug it so his legs wouldn't have to be folded up. I wanted him to be able to stretch out like me and him was running rabbits. I opened his eyes wide so he could see where he was going.

I couldn't think of the words you're suppose to say, but I tied two sticks together with bailing wire for a cross. After the burying, I headed to the house to wash up. Granny had been watching through the screen door while she boiled beans on the stove with hog meat. When I walked in, she turned back to the stove and dabbed at her eyes with a dishtowel. She didn't look my way or say nothing. A wisp of wood smoke hung in the air that made my eyes water too.

I washed using soap, but I couldn't get the smell of Buster off me. I went ahead and did my face good. I didn't feel like listening to no fuss about it. When I came back to the kitchen, Leon was already home. He sat in one of the kitchen chairs with Granny standing in front patting his head, his face buried in her stomach. Hearing the bathroom door slam shut, he wiped his eyes and snotty nose on her apron.

"You killed Buster," he snarled.

"He needed killin'," I said.

When Leon made like he was going to lunge at me, Granny cuffed him on an ear with the palm of her hand, like only a mother knows how to do, so your ear rings long after. Leon's head slunk down between his shoulders as his eyes crept up to Granny's face to see if anything else was coming. The way Granny's eyes bore into him, there would have been if he'd so much as opened his mouth.

"We're beholden to you, Bud," Granny said.

Million Dollar Baby

Arnold marched into the office and locked his heels in front of the metal desk. Major Marshal glanced up from a stack of papers only long enough to recognize who entered.

"Lieutenant Broom. What's so all-fired important you've got to see the executive officer first thing Monday morning?"

The wings were already in Arnold's hand. He didn't want to fumble with nervous fingers taking them off his blouse while the major watched. He placed the wings in the center of the desk before returning his eyes to the wall behind the major's head.

The major pushed back in his chair. "What's this all about?"

"Sir, I won't fly anymore, sir." Arnold yelled it the way Marines yell everything.

"What the fuck are you talking about? You numbnuts." His booming voice quieted the chatter of the clerks outside the open door. The major glared, the heat of his temper filling the room, "Do you realize what you're saying?"

"Sir, I can't bomb. There's no need wasting more money."

"It costs a million bucks to train a pilot to your level. It's a little late in the game to be saving the taxpayers' money. Besides, the practice range gives you the best scores in the whole squadron. Of course you can bomb."

"Sir, I won't bomb."

"Are you saying that if I ordered you to hit a real target, you would refuse?"

"Sir, yes sir."

The major scooted his chair back to open the center drawer of the desk. He pulled out a .45 automatic and placed it beside

Arnold's wings. "If we were in-country right now, I'd give you a chance to do just that."

"Sir, yes sir."

"Yes sir, what?"

"You'd shoot me dead, sir."

"You're damn straight I would." He picked up the wings and shook them at Arnold. "Do you know what these wings represent?" He slapped them down beside the .45 and leaned back in his chair. "Tradition. Tradition, goddammit! Do you know how many Marines have died proudly wearing these wings?"

Arnold glanced down at the gold wings and the blued steel pistol, the stark contrast of honor beside death—yet undeniable harmony. When Arnold's eyes rose, the Samurai sword framed against red velvet on the wall behind the major became a blur.

"Sir, I can't support the war anymore."

"Can't support—who gives a shit? Your opinions don't mean crap. We've got generals a hell-of-a-lot smarter than you to do the thinking."

Arnold checked his posture—shoulders back, chest out—determined not to wilt under the contempt he knew was coming.

"You been listening to that Cronkite shit? Somebody ought to shoot that traitor son-of-a-bitch. Listen, we're winning this war. You think we're gonna waste thousands of Marines and not win?"

The major's scowl dared Arnold to answer.

"You feeling sorry for the gooks, that it? We're fighting for their freedom, democracy. And even if we don't win, them gooks will be better off anyway. Look at Korea ... "

The major stopped abruptly and slammed the desk with the heel of his fist. "You shithead. Get out of my office. As a matter of fact, I want you out of my squadron. Don't even go back to the ready room. You don't deserve to be in the company of real Marines. When this gets out, they'll avoid you like a turd." He pointed first at Arnold and then the doorway. "I'll transfer you to some headquarters' support group. You sit in the chair outside my door until I can get the paperwork approved. I want you in that seat every minute until I get new orders. Any questions, Lieutenant?"

"Sir, no sir."

"Dismissed."

Arnold sat his body at attention beside the door, unseeing eyes rigidly ahead. When the major slammed the door, the eyes of the clerks lingered on Arnold before returning to their reports. A Corporal brought him coffee; later, a PFC returned with a box lunch from the mess hall.

After that, Arnold evaporated into thin air.

* * *

Three months earlier, Lieutenant Broom had been with the PF Flyer four miles up demonstrating the loops and Immelmanns on the final checkout ride before receiving his wings. He'd done the entire set of maneuvers required to prove he could fly a twin-engine jet while his instructor laughed and whooped in the seat beside him like a kid in a backyard pool. Arnold ended with a slow victory roll.

"By damn, I think you've got it. Some things can't be taught. You've either got it or you don't." PF laughed into the intercom connecting their helmets. "The Tweet is the funnest plane in the whole inventory. You'll have to leave it behind forever after this flight. An F-4 will feel like flying a brickbat after a Tweet. We've got some time to kill before our ETA. Whatcha want to do for an encore?"

"Spin recovery."

"By damn, Dumb Shit, you son-of-a-bitch."

It was Captain Wert in the ready room if brass was around, but PF in the air. He'd cleared that up when Arnold had called him *sir* during their first preflight together. *I ain't never fucked a white whore, so I ain't your daddy. We won't have time for this military happy-horseshit in the air. My handle is Pig Fucker, PF for short. From now on, you're Dumb Shit.*

"Come on PF, I know you've done it. If I don't do it now, I'll never do it."

The T37 trainer is the only military jet capable of recovering from a spin. The training manual explains the last-ditch maneuver although practicing it is strictly forbidden. *If recovery fails on the first attempt*, the manual says in a red warning note ballooned in the margin, *eject above 2000 feet AGL.*

"I can't do it without breaking an oath to the Skipper, but that ain't stopping you." The pitch of PF's voice rose with excitement. "Put her in a sixty-degree climb; throttles at sixty percent. She'll flame out if you don't keep the power up—found that out the hard way. Keep the nose up as long as the plane will fly. When it falls over, keep the stick back until the spin starts. Then recover like it says in the book."

The plane bucked trying to stay alive and then slid helplessly backward on its tail. The nose hammered over. The plane fluttered like a falling leaf. As he floated weightless against the tether of his seat harness, Arnold's body didn't sense up or down anymore. Patches of fields and forests began to swirl in the windscreen.

"Opposite rudder," PF yelled into the intercom. "Push the stick forward and give it full rudder." He had redundant controls on his side of the plane but let Arnold figure it out. "Now keep the nose down until you have enough airspeed to fly. If you induce another spin pulling out, we're done."

The plane awoke and started flying again with three thousand feet to spare. If they'd started the maneuver at less than ten thousand feet, they wouldn't have made it. As Arnold turned toward the field, the adrenaline left them giddy and their attempts to talk trailed off into cackles. "Better let Approach Control know we're coming," PF was finally able to say. "If you brag about this and it gets out, they'll have my wings and I'll have your ass. Damn you. You're a sorry son-of-a-bitch to talk me into that."

Arnold made the call and was routed over the town of Selma. "Wasn't too hard, Pig Fucker. Wish we had the fuel to climb back up and do it again." They went back into the uncontrollable snigger of boys with expensive toys until they reached pattern altitude of twelve hundred feet. Arnold scanned the sky for other bees hovering around the hive.

PF's helmet jerked from side to side, looking out to the wings and craning around to look behind. He was fearless in the rarified air above twenty thousand feet, but anxious close to the ground. Arnold could hear the hiss of his breath on the intercom increasing to panic. His hands clenched into fists in his lap as he fought the urge to grab the stick and jump back up to safety.

Arnold made the usual perfect landing and tied down the plane. By the time they entered the debriefing room, PF was back to his chatty self. Rather than reviewing their final flight together, PF wanted to make sure he had imparted the fine art of romance he'd learned as a boy on a Midwestern farm.

"The secret is cowboy boots. When you slip their hind legs down in the cowboy boots ... " Arnold had heard all this many times, whenever PF ran out of tall tales. For PF, every second had to be filled with talking or doing with no time left over for thinking. "Damn boy, let's cut this sow loose and do some celebrating."

Arnold rode on the back of PF's trail bike to the Officer's Club. PF downed two quick drafts before hanging his head and staring into his mug. "Damn, I could get used to this."

Arnold watched PF's vacant face in the mirror behind the bar. The imprint of his helmet still glowed pink on his sweaty forehead. PF was fresh out of Nam. Rumor was he'd been sent back early to dry out in the Training Command.

"I saw Daisy Cutters on our wings today," he said. Daisy cutters, PF had told him, were bombs designed to explode on impact, sending out a chain that mowed the jungle to ankle height in a large enough circle for a helicopter to land. He'd carried them on anti-personnel missions as well. *You can clip the gooks' feet off without actually killing them. The grunts get a kick outta that shit.*

"And I saw Selma burning when we were coming in. Plumes of Napalm rose like hellfire right up to our elevators." He banged the empty mug on the bar for a refill. "Can't get that crap outa my head—can't tell what's real no more."

"There's got to be a way. Get some help."

"Hell no. If a Flight Surgeon knew what's going on between my ears, he'd pull my ticket for sure. Can you imagine me not flying? Can you think of anything worse?"

PF finished the third beer without lowering the mug. His eyes became half-lidded. "You'll be in-country in a couple of months. You'll fly every day and get to play with live ordinance. When you're off duty, you can have all the drugs and pussy you can stand. You'll love it."

He took a deep breath and held it a moment before letting it hiss out through his teeth. "There's nothing to worry about. Dying's quick and easy for a Marine pilot. You won't get past *oh-shit* before it's over. No bleeding-out in a rice paddy like a ground-pounder with his legs blown off. If you make it back, you'll still have all your body parts."

PF's eyes clenched and a shudder shook his shoulders. "All the crap I've done, all the people I've killed—wouldn't matter if I'd never come home. All accounts would be settled and the slate wiped clean. Dead men don't have regrets. Hell, my mother would remember me as a hero rather than a screwed-up drunk."

* * *

"Lieutenant Broom, get your ass in here," the major yelled through the open door.

Arnold reformed from ether and marched into the office and stood as before with his eyes on the sword. "Sir, yes sir." He tried to match the gruff loudness of the major.

"Shut the goddamn door."

Arnold obeyed and returned to stand at attention.

"At ease, lieutenant."

The major waited until Arnold looked down. He patted a packet of papers with his left hand. "This is your transfer to MABS-31. You're going to be their new Drug Abuse Officer. You'll be flying a desk and watching men piss in a bottle for the rest of your hitch if that's what you want."

Arnold stared at the sheaf of papers on the desk beside his wings, the debt to be paid.

"Lieutenant, this morning never happened. You had a bad day. Anybody can have a bad day. Pick up these wings and get the fuck back to the ready room. I've scheduled you for an air-to-air combat training mission at 1600 hours. All this will look different to you tomorrow."

The Christmas Present

The usual fake tree in the parlor had ropes of confetti-like paper wound around it and all the ornaments—praying hands, angels and such—Granny had been given over the years. No real tree was allowed in her house. She had ruled aluminum foil tinsel was too messy also, so there was never none of that. Momma said the tree looked exactly the same as when she was a kid, except that a strand of electric lights had been added after the house was wired. The lights were the shape of candles and little bubbles would rise in the candle shafts when they got warmed up.

In previous years, we'd opened the presents in front of the tree, but this year Gramps was bedridden, so we did it in his bedroom next to the parlor. Momma figured this would be his last Christmas.

I got to be Santa Claus last year and give out the presents. But this year, Leon thought his son, who he bragged had learned to read, should do it. At twelve, I was getting too old to be Santa Claus anyway, so it didn't matter none to me.

Leon married this woman named Rose a few months back who already had a boy and a baby girl. Momma said neither of the daddies would marry her—that she was white trash, but as good a woman as Leon would ever get. Leon, Momma's brother, lives right across the road in one of Gramps's tenant houses. I like Aunt Rose all right, and the kids too. Leon won't let me play with the kids—says I'm too rough and will make them mean. But Aunt Rose lets me babysit when Leon's at work and she wants to go somewhere.

For Christmas, Momma bought Granny a new picture for the parlor wall on account of the other picture got tore somehow. The old picture was of this little girl in a blue dress and white bonnet leading a milk cow into a barn. The tear made it look like the cow's head was cut off. Momma bought her a picture in a gold frame of a bunch of kids playing hopscotch in a schoolyard. Granny was beside herself pleased. When they took the old picture down to replace it, they found out about the termites. The old picture wasn't torn at all but eaten by the termites that were in the wall. When Leon came, he punched around on the wall with his finger and said he didn't figure nothing was holding that wall up except the wallpaper.

Granny shushed him and waved us all to the kitchen. She didn't want Gramps to know nothing about the termites or he'd worry himself even sicker. Leon said after Gramps died, he'd move Granny into a trailer over behind his place and burn this old house. Granny left out to the garden. She don't let nobody see her cry.

Momma punched Leon in the stomach and called him some names I'd never heard her use before. Aunt Rose was mad at Leon too, but Momma told me later it was on account of Aunt Rose had been sugaring up Granny so Granny would will the property to Leon. Momma overheard Aunt Rose tell Leon that it would only be fair after them taking care of her and Gramps. Momma said she could see right through that hussy.

So, I lay on the pallet babysitting Elizabeth, Aunt Rose's baby, while she slept. I was dozing, watching the bubbles in the tree lights and listening to them opening presents in the other room, when Elizabeth let out a scream.

"Bud!" Momma yelled out.

"I didn't do nothing," I yelled back.

"Check to see if she needs changing."

I didn't want to know. I'd seen Aunt Rose run her finger inside a leg of the diaper to check, but I wasn't doing that. I figured I'd just undo the safety pin and see for sure and then yell for help if there was some bad stuff. When I folded down the diaper, there wasn't the poopy smell I'd feared, but she was wet. Elizabeth quit crying when the cool air hit her bottom.

I got to thinking how this was the first time I'd seen a naked female, so I should figure things out. There weren't no pee-pod, or the likes as that. There was a spot where there should have been something, but there was nothing but a crease. I was more than a little bit disappointed.

"She's wet," I called back.

Aunt Rose showed up with a fresh diaper. "Go on in the bedroom," she said.

Gramps was sitting up in bed with a pile of presents in his lap. He'd been watching Aunt Rose's boy open his Christmas presents—toys and candy—and was grinning expectantly. There were big boxes and long boxes all done up in different paper and bows. Leon took the ribbon off the biggest present and handed it to Gramps. The old man barely had the strength to tear the paper off.

Inside his first present, there was another box also wrapped in shiny paper. When he finally got inside that box, there was a third box. Finally, after struggling it open, a foil pouch of Beech-Nut chewing tobacco fell out. He went through this again with the next present and again it was three boxes with chewing tobacco in the last one.

"Beech-Nut. Ain't that you favorite, Daddy?" Aunt Rose said walking in with Elizabeth on her hip. Aunt Rose had taken to calling Gramps "daddy." "We had so much fun wrapping them last night, didn't we Leon?" Leon didn't say nothing. I bet he didn't do none of the wrapping. Aunt Rose and her boy were giggling when Leon handed Gramps the next present.

Gramps just stared at it and his eyes got teary before they shut.

"You all come on out to the kitchen now," Granny said. "Daddy's gettin tired with all these goings-on. Let him get a little nap now. You kids want some peach pie?"

Without opening his eyes, Gramps raked the rest of the presents off the bed onto the floor.

"Come on now; we'll get some peach pie." Granny herded us all out of the room. We all sat around the kitchen table except Leon, who paced around with Elizabeth pressed to his shoulder.

"He didn't have to do that, did he?" Aunt Rose's voice cracked, and her eyes started to tear up.

Leon came up behind her and patted her back. "Now Rose, you know how he is. You know you shouldn't take this personal."

"He's not grateful at all for the presents—after all the hard work I put into wrapping them."

"Now Rose—"

"After buying Christmas for the kids, there wasn't hardly nothing left. Tobacco was all we could afford. I thought he'd understand that. And what can you buy for somebody that lies in bed all the time? Tobacco's about all you can get him that he can use."

"It's the dementia," Momma remarked. "Give him a break."

"He's just tired, Rose; don't make—" Leon started to say.

"What a thing for the kids to see, throwing the presents on the floor like that. What'll they think? They'll never get over being so embarrassed." Aunt Rose put her hands to her face and started sobbing.

"Just shut up about it, won't you?" Momma said and gave Leon a look. "Make her shut up."

Granny got up and busied herself cutting slices of the peach pie at the stove. I thought she might go back out to the garden if this kept up.

I left back to the bedroom while they continued the jabbering in the kitchen. Gramps shut his eyes pretending to be asleep when he saw somebody was coming in.

"It's just me, Gramps," I told him. His eyelids parted just slightly to verify there weren't nobody with me before he opened his eyes.

I lay the Roy Rogers model cap gun I got for Christmas on the patchwork quilt that covered all but his arms. He gave me a quizzical look when I shoved it close to his hand and he shoved it back.

"It's loaded," I told him and pushed it back to his hand again. He looked hard at me like he thought I'd gone crazy. Then the faintest smile of understanding crept onto his face. He grabbed the gun and stuck it under the quilt.

I went out and sat on the front porch swing. The window to Gramps' room faced the porch. It was cracked a little so I could hear fine.

It started with a scream, Aunt Rose, I think. Then there was the "bam, bam, bam" of the cap gun and then some more screaming.

I hightailed it to the barn. It wouldn't take them long to figure out where that cap gun came from.

The Snake God

One klick past the sultry dark of no-man's-land, firelight flickers onto the jungle canopy. Could be a mama-san's cook fire in the village—or gook patrol preparing a dawn attack. If NVA sappers, they will have mortars to turn the landing zone into Swiss cheese. He listens intently for voices, the mechanical clanks of weapons being moved into position. Nothing.

A muzzle flashes on the far side of the perimeter. The bullet thuds against a water buffalo behind him and reverberates like a gong. Another flash—an SKS Carbine from the sound of it. The same sniper from the previous night, the one assigned to keep the company from sleeping. To his front, the distinct click of an M-16 being switched to auto. The sentry is ready this time and sprays a clip into the blackness. The Marine thirty yards down the line does the same, and then the one down from him. A phosphorous flare pops and fizzes like static as it drifts down, tinting the swirling mist orange and glinting off the razor wire.

When the flare dies, he floats in total blackness, still facing the jungle he cannot see. The impending strike plays out in his mind. The first sign of their approach will be contrails if coming in high or smutty exhaust fumes if low. Over the crackle of radio static, a labored voice will report a call sign and position. After identifying himself as their forward air controller, the F-4's will be directed to an initial position south of the village to keep the sun's glare out of the pilots' eyes during their bomb runs. This also ensures their flight path will not be over the LZ in case they pickle early or late.

In front of hooches in the village, tiny bent women will look up from cook fires, searching the sky for the eerie growl. The lead aircraft will erupt from over the jungle in a shallow dive, napalm canisters tumbling, yellow flames blooming up behind. In the afternoon, he will tally the shriveled black bodies—the enemy killed-in-action for the report. His palms grind into his eyes.

If he can just divert his brain until the numbness of battle sets in. Girls, the sweet ones he had known as a teen, come to him in the order he had known them. Their innocent smiles turn to sneers. They hold signs; call him names. His fist bangs into a sand bag to drive them away. He retreats further into the past and becomes a barefoot boy on Gramps's farm.

* * *

Gramps sidestepped in the middle between two rows, taking quick, precise swipes, leaving little mounds with a single green shoot in the center. "First hoein' is when you do the thinnin'." He followed to Gramps' left, away from the backstroke of his hoe handle. "Just you watch. Proper corn hoein' can't be taught with words."

Movement caught his eye. A two-foot long green snake glided over the cornrows directly at him. He grabbed Gramps' overall leg. Gramps already had his hoe raised and redirected his strike to the snake. Each half writhed in the dirt, twirling and flipping. The shock brought on his need to pee and he stepped over a few rows. When he came back, the snake was still and Gramps had worked on down the row.

"Why'd that ole snake want to bite me, Gramps?"

"Ah Bud, that little feller was more scared than you were. It musta had a hole over yonder." Gramps waved his hand behind his back without looking. "He was just makin' a dash for cover and you were in his way." Gramps took a few more steps, a few more swipes, then fished a rag out of a back pocket and wiped his face. "You wuz afeared, weren't you, Bud?" He shook his head but Gramps didn't buy it. "That's the only reason I kilt it. Snakes would be our friends, if'n we let 'em. They's eat the bad critters what eat the corn."

Gramps reached the edge of the field, and as he hoed the next row, they came back by the snake. Ants crawled on its eyes. "Weren't fair," he told Gramps. He didn't know whether to blame Gramps, the snake, or himself. "Will it go to Heaven?"

"Naw, Bud—leastwise not the one we go to. Snakes got a different god than we do."

He'd scraped a hole with his foot between the rows to bury the snake pieces so he wouldn't have to see them again and think about it.

Snakes didn't scare him after that. If he spotted one, he'd pin it to the ground with a forked stick until he could grab it just behind the head. The snake might coil around his arm, but it couldn't bite if held properly. He'd take it to Gramps to learn what kind.

Gramps schooled him about the poisonous varieties. "Don't fool around with them that's head look like a plow point. They'll take a stand and fight. And they go in pairs. While you're catchin' one, the other one sneaks up on you."

One morning, he caught a baby snake, only eight inches long. He wasn't sure what kind, but even if it were poisonous, he figured it was too small to hurt anybody. Gramps was in the field, so he dropped it in a gallon lard can and put a piece of cardboard over the top. He punched holes in the cardboard with a pencil so the snake could breathe and left the can on the kitchen table 'till Gramps came in for lunch.

Gramps flopped down at the table while Granny laid out a plate of cold biscuits and ham. When she grabbed the bail of the lard can, the cardboard fell off.

"How'd this nasty bucket get on the table?" she asked Gramps.

She turned the can upside down and nested it on a stack of empty lard cans beside the stove. Gramps scratched his chin whiskers looking from the pail to the cardboard full of holes on the floor. His head snapped around with a scowl when he figured it out

"Lee," Gramps said to Granny's back. "There's a rain a comin'. Got no time for a sit-down." He broke apart a biscuit and inserted a ham slice. "Gonna need your help gettin' the corn hoed before them clouds let loose."

"So be it," Granny called back as she swung open the screen door, headed for the toolshed. He followed Gramps out, him walking slow while he finished his biscuit. When Granny disappeared into the toolshed, Gramps grabbed his arm with one hand and with the other lifted him off the ground with a wallop.

"Boy, you're gonna remember this day. If Lee finds out you let a snake loose in her kitchen, you and me will be frying corn cakes over an open fire for supper." Gramps shoved him back toward the house and he barely jerked away from his kick. "Now, get your butt back in that kitchen and find that snake!" When the tool shed door slammed, Gramps' head turned to give Granny a broad smile. His face was a snarl when he turned back to him. "What kind?"

"Don't know. Never seen one like it."

"You'll have to kill it then."

"It's just a baby. Can't I just take it back where I found it?"

"If it's a copperhead and it gets growed, it'll claim a territory and strike at anything walking past—the mule, or Granny if she ain't paying attention. And them kind don't give polite warnings like a rattlesnake."

"But it's probably a good snake—"

"We ain't taking that chance.

"Don't make me kill it, Gramps."

"Well then, throw it over in the hog pen. Hogs hate snakes. That way it won't be your doings."

While he searched, he imagined the snake god on top of a cloud, a giant golden cobra with a flared head hovering side to side over its coiled body, lightning shooting from its eyes. "Spare him," he prayed to the snake god.

It was scrunched in the corner behind the broom. The pigs came running when they saw the pail in his hand. He begged the little snake to make a run for it, but it didn't.

* * *

Blackness fades and the horizon emerges. Above, high clouds tint pink, then blood red. Launch is scheduled for sunup. At the hot pad a hundred miles away, two crews will be strapping in, the plane captains signaling as the J79 engines whir and moan. A half hour flight time and then ...

His eyes clinch before he escapes again.

* * *

The first time he had killed a snake with his own hands had been last August in base housing at Beaufort. His new wife ran into the garage.

"Snake!" she shrilled and clutched his arm.

He stood up from smearing Bondo over a dent in a '57 Chevy he'd bought at auction.

"Judy called—scared to death. It's in her front yard. Got her kids locked in the house till somebody kills it."

"What kind?"

"A snake, dammit! Judy says it's as long as a rake handle. Should I call the MP's?"

He got a pull handle from the toolbox and walked next door to Captain Smithson's front yard. The snake was big all right—a cottonmouth, a real beauty. It had a coke bottle size bulge midway like it had swallowed a rat and slithered across the manicured grass in lazy S-curves toward the slough on the far side of the street. He laid the steel rod at the back of the snake's head and it froze perfectly still. It would have been nothing to grab it and help it to its destination.

At the Smithson house, the kids' faces pressed against the picture window, Smithson behind calming his wife. It had to be done. They had to see the snake killed or Judy would never let the kids play in the yard again. "Forgive me," he begged the snake and clubbed the head as precisely as he could. As the bloody carcass thrashed on the lawn, he thought about fear, the awful tragedies fear can bring.

* * *

When the sun reaches a hand's width above the horizon, two F-4's emerge like gnats in the south sky. Now, with it inevitable, the numbness creeps in. Friend or foe no longer matters. Fire will purge everything—even the snakes. The jungle will recover from ash, and in a few years this will have never happened.

The Lesson

Ruby held her new sweater, already soppy with blood, against Sterling's face. With her free hand at his back, she pushed him through the doorway of the infirmary.

When Anita whirled from a filing cabinet, her hands rose to her chubby cheeks, her eyes wide with fright. "What on earth happened?" Her cringing face became pale as her squat body wobbled. It was a joke in the teacher's lounge that the school had hired a nurse who fainted at the sight of blood. While Anita recovered, Ruby clutched the back of Sterling's shirt and puffed at a blond strand of hair that had escaped her barrette.

Anita finally pointed to a straight-backed chair beside a gurney in the center of the room, "Sit here," she directed. "Hold your head back."

When Ruby pulled her sweater away from Sterling's face, drips of blood trickled from each nostril. She wiped the drips away roughly with a dry part of the sweater until the bleeding stopped. Anita steadied Sterling's head with her hands to his temples, away from the smears on his face, and peered up his nostrils as if expecting to see something.

Ruby ran cold water in the washbasin against the wall and dropped in her sweater. She didn't bother with the ruined sweater, but pumped disinfectant soap from a plastic bottle to wash Sterling off her hands.

"Was he in a fight? Wait, wait!" Anita jumped over to the phone and hit a quick dial number. "I'll have to get Principal Miller in here to hear this." After a moment, "Wait, wait, I'll have to page him." She punched another number and Cindy heard the ringing feedback of the intercom. "Principal Miller, please call—come to the infirmary. Principal Miller to the infirmary."

Ruby came back to make her own appraisal of Sterling's nose. She pinched his chin and twisted his head from side to side. Yep, it was broken all right, but nothing more. He'd be in one of those funny masks for a few days. Ruby glared down into Sterling's eyes thinking how the crooked nose would remind him of this day even years later. His eyes were teary, but Ruby suspected it wasn't remorse. She took some cotton pads out of a glass canister, moistened them with alcohol, and wiped the blood off his face so Anita wouldn't have to do it. Sterling's reproachful eyes followed her every move, but he didn't wince or pull back.

Over six feet, muscular from football, blond wavy hair, he was the heartthrob of every girl in school and the envy of every boy. He'd had it his way since kindergarten according to the scuttlebutt in the teacher's lounge. Although his impetuous behavior often got him in trouble, his prominent family had kept him clear of anything serious.

She cupped his chin in her palm, staring into the defiant eyes. She wasn't sorry for Sterling but for herself. This was the end of teaching for her. She could explain that what she did was justified, but in the end, it wouldn't matter. If asked, she'd admit it was a coldly calculated act she didn't regret. Knowing that this puppy-faced boy had brought her down made her want to punch him again.

A tentative smile crept onto Sterling's face. She couldn't help but smile back. After all, he was a victim too, not of her, but the hormone-tainted blood blustering through the brains of all boys his age. She couldn't bring herself to hate him.

Ruby pulled a chair from the wall to beside Sterling and waited. Principal Miller was a fair man who she respected. He would ask the questions he had to ask, and she would answer truthfully. Who knows what Sterling would say? She wouldn't dispute anything. There was no need for further drama. After all, she was a first-year student teacher and Sterling was the son of a judge, the school's football hero. The outcome was inevitable so she would just endure what was about to happen and be done with it. She wasn't teacher material anyway.

"What's going on?" Principal Miller wanted to know as he rushed in and propped his lean frame against the gurney bed. He looked back and forth between the faces waiting for a reply and then settled on Anita. "What's going on here?"

"Sterling's got a broken nose, I think."

"What do you mean 'you think'?"

"Well, I'd rather let a doctor do a thorough examination—."

"Anita, I can see from here he's got a broken nose. I need to know how it happened."

Again, Principal Miller looked from one of them to the other and nobody spoke. This time his gaze stopped at Ruby. "What happened?"

Ruby went through it in her mind, weighing how awful it would sound, hoping she wouldn't cry. Sterling had malingered after her class until he was the last to leave the room. As she was erasing the assignment off the blackboard, he had brushed her rear with his hand. She had frozen at first, thinking it was inadvertent, but then his fingers explored further. When she spun around, he jumped back with a mischievous grin as he continued out the door. She had gone to the threshold and called his name as he meandered away. When he turned, he still had the self-satisfied grin. She found herself smiling back, playfully beckoned him with her finger. She went back into her room, leaving the door open, and leaned against her desk. She didn't think he would actually come back, but he did. What did he think he was going to get?

He watched her close the door, returning her flirtatious smile. He towered over her when she walked up to him, her head tilted back as if inviting a kiss. As his head bent forward, she precisely placed her uppercut to the tip of his nose. She stood her ground with fists clenched, but he fell into a ball at her feet writhing in pain. When he sat up, the blood drooled onto the waxed linoleum.

"Well, Miss Love?" Miller asked impatiently.

Ruby was shifted in her seat, dreading the sound of her voice, when Sterling gurgled something.

Miller turned to him, "Yes Sterling?"

Sterling lowered the blood-splotched icepack he held to his nose, but it still sounded like he was talking underwater. "Walked into a door." He tilted his head back and replaced the compress, his eyes locked on Miller, judging if he had been convincing.

Miller looked incredulous, "You walked into a door?"

Sterling's head nodded. Miller looked to Ruby who quickly looked at the floor hoping he wouldn't ask her to confirm it.

"Our star football player broke his nose walking into a door?" Miller's eyes demanded more.

Sterling's sheepish grin and the *shit-happens* hump of his shoulders resolved Miller's doubts.

"Boy, from now on I want you to wear your helmet everywhere you go," he chortled. "As it is, you'll miss the next game. Anita, call the Judge and tell him to come pick up his bumbling son and take him to a doctor. Tell him he got hurt at practice—no need in Sterling having to tell his daddy he did something so stupid. That okay with everybody?"

Ruby exchanged a sideways glance with Sterling.

"Ruby, you look a little pale," Miller said. "I'll bet this scared you to death. It's just one of those things that you'll learn to deal with when you're a teacher."

An Alternate Reality

Dust rising from the dirt road streams behind the car like a contrail.

"Damn. Who's coming to haunt me now?"

You park in the yard and step out—slender, dishwater hair like hers. After studying my adobe house and old pickup with the airplane painted on the side, you lean against your car and consider driving away.

The doorbell rings. Doorbells are for strangers, bill collectors. I've been expecting you. If the door were not open, I'd pretend not to be home.

"Who's there?"

You cup your hands around your eyes and try to peer past the screen.

"Are you Teddy?"

Nobody has called me Teddy in twenty years. I come to the screen for a better look. Last time you were a knobby-kneed kid with slightly crooked teeth like mine. I can't remember your name—purged from memory. *"Teddy?"* You ask again without a 'good morning' or even a smile. You know who I am. You look at my face comparing my features to your own.

"Who are you looking for?"

I don't want you here—not after so long. You can tell from my voice you're not welcome and glance back at your car, think again about leaving, then back to me.

"My father."

I try not to appear shocked. I push open the door, seat you at the Formica table, and pour stale coffee.

"How did you find me?"

"A letter. This address was on the envelope of a letter mother never mailed—and a journal you must have written. I found them in her things."

"She's dead?"

Your eyelids flicker in acknowledgment. I walk to the kitchen window, prop stiff-armed on the sink, look into the garden. Suicide. She must have battled depression until the end. The skipper's wife, our confidante back then, called this morning; knew I'd want to know.

"Yeah, I gave that journal to your mother" ... after we knew Robert was coming home. I read her the part where we first met so she would know it had been real for me; that I hadn't tried to deceive her. We agreed she would burn it—as a symbol.

I turn and lean back against the counter, sip coffee, pretend absurdity. "What? You think I'm your father?"

Your face grows pink with rage. *"I'll leave if you want."* You've anticipated my denial, rehearsed your response, promised yourself not to make a scene.

"Your father's in California—an invalid" ... blind, his face burned away before you were born. Margo was two, a baby when he last saw her. The man you grew up calling daddy was a grotesque husk of the man I knew. You would have closed your eyes before entering his room, faced the window while reading him Dr. Seuss.

"He loved you. He loved your mother. Your mother loved him."

"She loved a man she knew before I was born. That's what I want from you, to know who he was—before."

"Yeah, I knew him in Nam" ... and your mother from the letters. He felt sorry for a bachelor and let me read her letters— mostly stuff about Margo.

"He was my wingman when he was shot down" ... one SAM, two exhausts to follow. It chose him. Captured, taken to the North for a year.

"Then you know he's not my father."

Your eyes follow my gaze to the cupboard door. Behind it is the bottle still half full.

"All I have is rum … and Coke. How about a rum and Coke?"

"My father is a drunk."

* * *

Mission Control knew them as Eagle Flight, two A-4's in route to an X on a map. Pulling out from my bomb run, I pushed the mic button. "Eagle One—off target."

"Eagle Two—on target," came the response. Over my shoulder, I saw Robert's Skyhawk turn on its side and the nose fall into a sixty-degree dive. Tracers rose to greet him.

"We lit up something," Robert reported when he pulled out. "Have you in sight at my ten o'clock."

I reduced throttle to 80 percent and flew level so Robert could catch up and we could fly home in formation. Robert drifted to my wing, his face hidden behind the shaded visor of his helmet. He was signaling a thumb-up with his throttle hand when his plane disintegrated into a smudge of black smoke. A SAM, a heat-seeker launched after the first bomb run, had found Robert first.

If there were a second missile, I'd have to outmaneuver it. In the 6-G turn, my sagging oxygen mask pinched off breathing. Even with the G-suit inflated to max, everything past the instrument panel was a blur. I relaxed the turn just long enough to roll inverted and see the smoke plume of Robert's plane in the jungle, then pulled hard again until the blue of the Gulf of Tonkin came into my windscreen. No more dodging. I pressed the throttle hard against the stop and dove for the treetops. There was barely enough fuel for a balls-out run. The ack-ack rounds exploded around my canopy.

* * *

The neck of the rum bottle rattles against the glass in my hand. I collapse into a kitchen chair, hyperventilating the way I had that day. You look at the terror in my eyes and wonder.

"He was the best man I ever knew."

* * *

When my tour was up, I'd found her living in base housing. Robert's official status was MIA since his body had not been recovered. I wanted to tell her how her husband had died a hero; how much he'd loved her—a gesture for a dead comrade, consolation for his widow.

Six months later, your mother and I watched Cronkite on TV. A gurney rolled down the ramp of a C-130 in Saigon, a dying man the North had thrown in for free during a prisoner exchange, his head bandaged, still in his flight suit, squadron patch visible on his shoulder. I'd known then, before the base chaplain rang her doorbell.

We'd met his plane at Dulles, rode in the ambulance with him to Walter Reed. She was already visibly pregnant to everyone but him. The words from behind the bandages were garbled. "The dream of us together kept me alive." She'd held his hand, limp from morphine, and looked at me. "I love you," she'd said.

That night I hopped a C-130 flying south to Key West with a refueling stop at our base at Beaufort. I packed my shave kit and the change of class-A's, all I'd brought with me to her house—his house. Later, when he was stronger, she would tell him about the baby. Everything. They would cry together. He would forgive her, but never me.

A NATO exercise in the Mediterranean left me with one month to go on my enlistment. A talented corporal from Airframes painted an A-4 on the door of my new pickup and I drove west. In Taos, New Mexico, an old Indian asked me what it was. That's when I bought this run-down ranch.

* * *

"You came here once" … on the way to San Diego, to the hospital where Robert had been transferred for treatment. She had you and Margo with her. You were maybe six. "You wouldn't remember."

A drink glass bangs on the table. You put your face squarely in front of mine. *"I remember. I remember the desert and a dusty cowboy that smelled like shit and never shaved."*

"You got your mother's looks, thank goodness, but your mother could never be that cruel."

"You're right. You knew her pretty well. The meanness comes from my father."

Considering the extent of his injuries, Robert shouldn't have lived long. As months turned into years, I lay awake nights willing him to die. In alcohol-fueled stupors, I made trades with God, the Devil, whoever would listen, to let him die—let my best friend die.

"You have no concept of mean."

"I'm going now. I just wanted you to know I hate you."

"Don't leave me alone … not today."

Follow me into this bottle; we can reset the past to what it should have been. Robert died in Nam and I raised our two daughters; or the missile killed me instead. If one of us had died that day, your mother would have had the big family she wanted, backyard barbecues, and country club dances with her husband.

Your father would have attended doll tea parties, watched your dance recitals, and stood by your side at your wedding. In these alternate worlds, your father bounces grandbabies on his knee, and you kiss him on the cheek when he says he loves you.

Gallup

The guy rattled on. "There's really no difference between the Indians and the Mexicans out here. In the US, we killed off most of the Indians, and what was left we herded onto reservations. But in Mexico—and this used to be part of Mexico—the Spanish assimilated the Indians. They thought Indians were regular people, like you and me."

Bud slumped in the passenger seat; eyes rigidly ahead, nodding to show he was paying attention like he did in Misses Griffith's fourth period history class. The tires whop-whopped across several seams of the concrete highway before the man spoke again.

"In a lot of ways, the Indians were more civilized than the Spanish. I mean the Indians treated the Spanish like gods and they destroyed their cities anyway—culture, everything. Anyway, when the conquering part was over, they took the remaining Indians as slaves to dig for gold and such. So, the Spanish soldiers started breeding the squaws and that's how you come up with Mexicans. There are no more Spanish and no more Indians around here, only Mexicans."

Bud at first tried to keep up his side of a conversation, the usual pay for a hitchhiker, but a few miles out of Albuquerque it was obvious this man only wanted an audience for his endless babble. The man had said his name when he picked him up, but Bud instantly forgot it. After the man dropped him off in Flagstaff, he never wanted to see him again.

It was a lucky hitch, however, halfway to his destination of the Grand Canyon, so he wouldn't do anything to piss him off. And the ride was nice, a red 1964 Jaguar convertible, still with the new-car smell. The man had bragged about all the bells and whistles as they drove out of Albuquerque. Bud wished he could just listen to Mexican music on the radio.

The guy rambled on. "And the Spanish, they're a half breed race anyway. Back in the Middle Ages, Arabs out of Africa invaded Spain, and after a few centuries, the Europeans blood was tainted by the Arabs. And the Arabs—what race are they anyway? A mixture of Chinks, Jews, and Negros … "

Bud watched the desert streaming past the right window, endless sand with sporadic sagebrush and yucca. Out of the corner of his eye, he could see the man glancing at him, maybe expecting him to say something. Bud didn't know anything about Arabs other than they rode camels. He was relieved when the lecture continued.

"You see those boulders out there?"

Bud did wonder about the elongated rocks, striated bluish-grey, and yellow, seeming misplaced in the buff flat expanse. They were the only things breaking the horizon besides those cacti that resembled men waving.

"Those are petrified logs. This all used to be jungle way back, and when it dried up, the trees fossilized into rocks. If you look closely, you can see the growth rings on some of them. Hard to imagine this as a lush jungle with dinosaurs and such, huh?" The man paused and glanced at Bud as if waiting for a response.

"They don't look like trees, at least not no more."

For the first time, he appraised the appearance of the driver—middle aged, tan, thinning brown hair carefully combed to the rear to cover a bald spot and held in place with thick tonic. The wind fluttered a loose-fitting Hawaiian shirt about his pudgy body. He couldn't see his eyes behind the mirrored sunglasses. His constant grin, Bud figured, was calculated to put others at ease—a traveling salesman of some sort.

Bud's mind drifted when the guy finally shut up. The arrow-straight highway zipped beneath them at seventy miles per hour, but outside the window nothing changed, as if this part of the world wasn't governed by time and distance.

Bud pulled the post card from his shirt pocket where he always carried it. The picture was creased and worn, the corners dog-eared, but he could still make out the orange and yellow buttes of the Grand Canyon with the bright green Colorado slithering through like a garden snake. On the flip side in his mother's scrawl he read, "Dear Bud, Having a wonderful time here with Frank. Wish you could see this. Back in a few days. Mom." He held the postcard to his nose and thought he could smell her. She might still be there, he thought, or maybe somebody could tell him—

"Do you like girls?"

Bud was startled back into the car. "Mostly" he replied, wondering where that question was headed. "Depends on the girl, I guess."

"I mean, do you like 'em? You've been with girls, right?"

"Of course." This was a lie. He'd never even held hands with a girl, but this guy wouldn't know that.

"Well, did you like it?"

"Yeah. Nothin' better than rubbing on titties." Bud figured this was prelude to the man bragging about some conquest, but the guy remained quiet until they came to the outskirts of Gallup.

From the travel guide he had found at the Raton train station, Bud knew Gallup, at the New Mexico and Arizona border, was the only town on Route 66 between Albuquerque and Flagstaff. Also, that it is in the middle of the desert and surrounded by Indian reservations. Filling stations and one-story buildings made taller with false facades lined the highway. Abandoned cars without tires clogged the alleys. Down the side streets, stucco houses with brightly colored trim sat behind sand yards walled with stacked stone. The windows, opaque with a film of grimy dust, flashed reflections of the low sun.

The car slowed onto the shoulder of the road, "This is as far as we go, Bud."

"You said you were goin' to Flagstaff."

"Nope, Gallup is as far as I go." He motioned to the passenger door with the back of his hand.

Bud retrieved his quilted jacket from the floorboard. Everything he owned was stuffed in the pockets. He'd lost his cap out the back of a pickup between Raton and Cimarron. After Bud stepped out, the guy reached across and shut the door before Bud could turn around. The man sped to a filling station a block ahead and turned back east, accelerating past Bud without a glance. Bud shot him a finger in case the guy was looking in the mirror.

Lady Macbeth

Ruby holds to the pole and flashes a titillating smile over her shoulder while shimmying her booty. Past the footlights are silhouettes of men backlit by the bar. They sit on stools at small round tables sipping draft beer from plastic cups. The glare keeps her from seeing their faces, but she knows them, or men like them—truck drivers on their overnight stop between somewhere and somewhere else. The Bunny Hop is strategically located within walking distance of the Flying J truck stop and Motel 6. For the most part, they are mild-mannered family men wanting nothing more than mindless diversion before winding down their day.

Against the back wall of the cavernous room, Harley waits at the light controls behind the bar for his cue in the Van Halen blare to switch on the strobe. The music slows and Ruby teases away the last layer of her costume leaving a G-string and the pasties tipped with tassels. The truckers, wanting the full experience, move to chairs at the foot of the stage. She dances closer to accommodate them.

With a dip of her shoulder, she starts the tassels twirling clockwise, faster and faster until they becomes the blur of airplane propellers. She stops rigid and lets them wind down before dancing around the pole and returning to repeat the same feat counterclockwise. The regulars know this is not the end and lean in even closer, some propping their elbows on the stage. She dances back and leans against the pole for balance before the footlights go out. She imagines the men holding to their seats in the darkness with the spectacle continuing in their minds. Light leaks from behind the curtain covering the dressing room door as the other girls come out to watch.

With her hands, she maneuvers her breasts to swing the tassels in opposite directions. Once started, they are as easy as a hula-hoop to keep going. The strobe light flicks on and she is at the edge of the stage. Her lime-green florescent G-string and matching tassels become heavenly bodies floating in a black universe. The heartbeat pulse of the strobe causes the whirling tassels to blink. "Aaahs" and "damns" come from the darkness. She resists twirling faster lest her boobs lose sync and crash together. The sudden disorientation has caused men to fall off their seats. With the ending twang of a guitar riff, the footlights blare again.

"Put your hands together for Lady Macbeth from Music City. Let's hear it for Macbeth," Harley announces over the PA. The applause is generous with a few catcalls. She acknowledges their appreciation with an exaggerated curtsy. As she bends to pick up the dollar bills left at the edge of the stage, a hand reaches out of the darkness to tuck a twenty under her G-string strap.

"We'll have a short intermission and then we will invite Coco to the stage." Harley pauses and looks to the curtain covering the dressing room door. "Coco? You're up next." An arm extends past the curtain and waves. The PA clicks off and the stage lights dim.

Ruby gathers up her costume pieces strewn on stage and slips behind the curtain. One more routine before heading home.

* * *

"Teach me," Coco pleads while Ruby reassembles the layers of her outfit. Ruby stares down at Coco's firm, perky tits.

"Cindy, you don't need stunts like that."

"Please..."

"Here." Ruby carefully peels off the pasties. "Take these and practice in front of the mirror. Don't get your hopes up. You're not built right."

Cindy compares Ruby's breasts to her own and pouts.

"I'd rather have what you've got, girl. After your first baby, you'll be floppy enough to make it work." Ruby leans forward to plant an assuring kiss on her forehead. "Even if you do learn, you'll never get a chance to use it—not on stage anyway. This time next month you'll be in a dorm room studying anatomy from a book."

Cindy smiles—not the frozen facade used on stage, but with irrepressible joy—the smile that blossoms whenever Ruby mentions college. The other dancers tease as Cindy dips and sways in front of the mirror trying to get the tassels to swing. Her giggles, a stark contrast to the trembling sobs of a month ago, flood Ruby with warmth. *She's gonna make it.*

* * *

It had been a sultry July afternoon. Ruby and Harley sat at the end of the bar by the propped-open door enjoying the breeze before opening time. A skinny girl in a shabby pleated dress walked out of the glare and stood slump-shouldered before them.

"I...I need a job."

"How old?" Harley asked.

"Twenty-one."

Harley frowned his disbelief. He twirled his fingers for her to turn around and she cowered under his glare. When she faced him again, her eyes glistened at the verge of tears and her straggly blonde curls trembled. Harley, of course, didn't notice and pointed to the stage.

"Can you dance? Want to show me what you can do?"

She looked over her shoulder at the stage and then down at her feet. "I don't know how." Without waiting for Harley's verdict, she walked like a rag doll back through the glare of the doorway.

"Harley, you're about as sensitive as a Brahma bull. You could have at least asked her name before putting her through your cattle-call routine."

Harley's face contorted into his *what-the-hell* expression before Ruby walked out into the parking lot. She found the girl sitting against the rear wall of the Bunny with her face hidden in the hem of her dress. Ruby quietly sat down beside her. When Ruby touched her shoulder, the girl flinched with a gasp.

"Now, now. Nobody's gonna hurt you." Ruby dug a tissue from her pocket and dabbed snot and tears from the girl's face. "You on the run?"

The girl glanced toward the parking pad at the Flying J. "I can't go back. I'm never going back."

"Got any place else to go?"

She looked down and slowly shook her head.

Ruby pulled the girl into a hug. "Us girls gotta stick together."

The girl sniffled in ragged jerks as Ruby finger-combed her hair. The girl's taut body seemed to melt and flow against her.

"Name's Ruby. Around here, I'm Macbeth. What's your name? How old are you really?"

"Cindy. Seventeen."

Ruby swayed as if soothing a baby, her own vision blurred from the sudden stab of pain. Her daughter would have been seventeen, had she lived.

"Cindy, do you trust me?"

The girl squirmed a nod against Ruby's chest.

"I live not far from here. Do you want to stay there until...?" Cindy vigorously nodded again.

* * *

She and Cindy had nested into each other's voids like puzzle pieces. Cindy needed the mother who had deserted her; Ruby needed her dead daughter back. As simple as that—analyzing it further became morbid and twisted.

Cindy never talked about what she had been fleeing that day. However, in the month they had lived together, hints leaked out in unguarded moments. Her father was a truck driver. Her mother had run away with another man. After she finished high school, her father sold their house and traded for a truck with a sleeper birth. Ruby had not pressed for details.

All the dancers at the Bunny hid sordid pasts too painful to touch. Asking someone's history obligated the asker to reciprocate. Ruby's backstory was off-limits also: the car wreck that killed her infant daughter, the paralyzing depression, the husband that drifted away, the other men who eventually dubbed her damaged goods. She now had reached the bottom, stripping at a watering hole beside the interstate to support a drug habit she had picked up along the way.

At first, afraid to be left alone at night, Cindy had stayed in the dressing room at the Bunny while Ruby worked. The other dancers took to her immediately, letting her try on their costumes and teaching her erotic dance steps. Two weeks later, Cindy became Coco, a struggling Vanderbilt student dancing for tuition. The story, along with her innocent pout on stage, translated into big tips from the fatherly truckers.

When Ruby corroborated Cindy's story to the truckers it felt authentic. Ruby imagined herself a mother nobly supporting her daughter's ambition the only way she could. Cindy had fallen into the fantasy also, calling her "Mom" when they were alone. If only these delusions could be made real.

Cindy could send for her high school transcript. If her grades were as good as she bragged, they would apply to a junior college. Ruby could become a teacher again, her job before the accident, and they would cram for the ACT before work. She would quit cold turkey her decade-old drug habit; Cindy would nurse her through withdrawal. They would start a college fund in a cookie jar. Together they would create a path out—at least for Cindy.

Ruby looks in the wall mirror and considers her own future. In the closed world of interstate trucking, she is legendary. Other strippers use tassels, but truckers laud she alone has mastered the counter-rotation twirl. Routes are carefully planned to overnight at the Flying J. New drivers ask Harley if this is the place where Lady

Macbeth performs. She leans toward the mirror to touchup the mask of makeup that is Macbeth's face and then stands back to appraise her overall look. Macbeth's career is waning. With her bum knee, she can no longer do the calisthenics on the pole. Just dancing three sets a night leaves her limping. Once she wore a knee brace, but Harley nixed that.

Fully reassembled and covered with a flimsy negligee, she puffs an atomizer of toilet water over herself before going out front to mingle with the customers. Most of the men she greets by name with a pat to their back. A familiar form sitting at a dark corner table catches her attention with a wave. Bar lights sheen off his slicked-back oily hair. She saves his table for last.

"Hello Chez. Must be a month since you've been here."

"People in Nashville looking for me. Skipped off to Kentucky for a while."

"Buy me a drink?"

"Sure. The usual—Crown and ginger?" He waves for the waitress and then points at Ruby.

She touches his hand clasped around a mixed drink. "Is this the hand that belongs to that twenty? Couldn't see your face from up there."

"Lots more where that came from. Brought you some good stuff. In the mood for a trade?"

Mary Lou brings her drink—straight ginger ale. Chez puts a ten spot on her tray.

When Coco is introduced and starts her seductive gyrations to a Jimmy Hendricks number, his eyes narrow as if grading cattle.

Ruby motions with her head toward the stage. "Coco's new, a pre-med student at Vanderbilt. Dances on the side for tuition money. If you've got an extra twenty, she could use the help."

"That so? Cute. Kinda young, but I bet she's trainable. How about introducing us. Who knows, we might become best buddies."

Ruby remembers being introduced to Chez by a fellow dancer when she first arrived at the Bunny, how he had played on her brokenness to hook her on drugs.

"Coco's off limits, Chez."

Chez picks up on her sternness and turns away from Coco to squint into Ruby's eyes. "What? You like her mother, or something?" When he reads the answer in Ruby's face, he sits back with a grin.

Ruby swings her slouch purse from her shoulder onto the table. "No more deals, Chez." She slides a twenty across to him. "Took the cure. Don't need your pills anymore."

He reaches for her drink and takes a swig. "Kinda weak." He leans forward with a glare. "Don't treat me like one of your trucker assholes. I know when a game's being played. Look at you—shaking like a leaf. You're still using. In the end, you know I'll get what I want. Either you or that bimbo up there—your choice."

Ruby takes her drink from his hand. "So Coco will be your new love interest—that what you're thinking?"

Chez stands at the end of Coco's routine. "That's exactly what I'm thinking." He exaggerates his clapping as he walks to the edge of the stage, leans past the footlights, and motions with a crooked finger for Cindy to come closer. When he pulls back the elastic of her G-string and lets it pop against a twenty, she winces but mouths, "Thank you."

Ruby spits in Chez's drink and puts it back on his coaster before he returns. "That was my last dance," she says getting to her feet, "Changed my mind about your offer. If it's still good, palm a bottle of percs into my purse."

Chez grins. "Now we're talking."

"Meet me in the parking lot in fifteen minutes."

Ruby carries her cup to the bar and motions to Harley for a refill. While Harley is busy, she reaches over the bar, grabs the knife used for cutting limes, and slips it into her purse. When

Harley brings her drink, she sighs. "Harley, I'm not feeling well. Need to skip the last dance."

"You ain't sick. What's going on?" Harley glares at Chez's table. "Thought you were past all that."

"Thought I was too."

Harley jerks erect, his face fierce, and his chest expanded like a gorilla. "Time I had a talk with that—"

"Harley, don't make this harder than it is. I am who I am. Fire me if you have to." She pecks his stubbly cheek before going backstage to dress.

* * *

Detective Duffy, tie askew, paunch straining his sweaty white shirt, stands in front of the bar in the spotlight of the setting sun thrown through the open door of the Bunny Hop. Harley flicks on the intercom. "Hey, Coco—need you up at the bar." Duffy follows Harley's gaze to the curtain at one side of the stage. Cindy's head emerges, hair in curlers. Harley waves her toward the bar.

"Let me change clothes first," she yells before disappearing.

Duffy checks his note pad. "Mister Harley—is that right?"

"Just Harley."

Duffy holds the picture on his cell phone in front of Harley. "So you've never seen this guy before?"

"Lot of men come through here. Looks sorta like a pill pusher I threw out about a month ago. Hard to tell with all that blood."

"Might fit. There was a satchel of pills in the room. Remember his name?"

"Naw. Don't keep track of names. Showed him the door when I figured out what he was up to. Don't allow no drugs in here."

Cindy walks up in a quilted bathrobe and a pink plastic shower bonnet covering her hair. She rests an arm on the bar and looks Duffy up-and-down with a frown.

"Coco, this here is Detective Duffy. Seems some guy got himself killed down at Motel 6. Found by one of those Mexican room cleaners about noon today. Wants to know if we know anything about it."

"Coco?" Duffy lays his phone on the bar and puts a pencil to his notepad. What's the last name?"

"Coco's her professional name," Harley intercedes. "Girls don't give out their real names."

Duffy looks between Coco and Harley.

Harley's hands come up palms toward Duffy. "We in trouble? Suspects or something? Need a lawyer—?"

"You can clam up; you've got that right. But I don't think you'll like how that plays out." Duffy folds his notebook and slips it back into his pocket. "You'll make yourself a suspect and I'll detain you for questioning. Vice gets called in and asks more questions—like if Coco is underage, for example. Homicide's not interested in any of that. If we keep this friendly and you give me honest answers, I'll be on my way."

"Cynthia White," Cindy says.

Duffy turns the cell phone screen to Cindy. "Do you know this guy?"

Cindy leans in and then jerks back aghast.

"I'm going to enlarge this so you only see his face. Take another look."

"Nope. Never seen him before. What happened to him?"

"Somebody slit his throat. Coroner says about midnight."

"Drug deal gone bad?" Harley asks.

"Could be, but not the usual. An addict wouldn't leave the drugs, or the money in his wallet." Duffy fingers the cell phone to bring up another picture. "And wouldn't have thought to wipe the murder weapon clean." He puts the picture of a stainless steel utility knife on the bar for them to see. "Ever seen this before?"

Harley looks closely at the picture, then at Cindy before answering. "How would I know? Got one just like it in my kitchen at home."

Cindy shakes her head.

"Who else was here last night?"

"House full of truckers. No telling where they are today."

"Staff? Dancers?"

"None of them here yet, except Coco. Look, Detective, if he had come in here, I'd know. I check everybody's ID when I collect the cover charge. Like I said, he wasn't here last night. Might ask around at the Flying J; maybe somebody saw him there."

Duffy digs in his coat pocket and places a business card on the bar in front of Harley. "Headed there now. I'll be back in a couple of hours when you're open." He turns to Cindy as he leaves. "Nice to meet you, Miss Coco."

Harley follows Duffy to the door and watches him pull away in an unmarked white sedan. When Harley turns back to the bar, he bumps into Cindy standing just behind him shivering. He pulls her to his burly chest.

"Cindy, I know this is scary, but it will blow over. You and Ruby need to disappear. Drive to Nashville or up into Kentucky. Do it right now. Don't ever come back."

He takes Cindy's shoulders in his hands and holds her at arm's length. "Where is she now?"

"Still in the shower when I left. Been in the shower off and on all morning. Scrubbed her skin raw." Tears dribble down Cindy's cheeks. "Says she can't get the smell of him off her."

Crystalina

As he passed through the edge of sleep, her face imprinted on his mind like a flash of lighting. Her eyes were the last to fade—bleary like when he last saw her, when it was finally over. Barney's eyes opened to blackness, heart pounding in his ears. The emotion of her lingered in the dark like a fragrance.

Had his arrhythmia or the torment of the dream caused his heart to race? It irritated him that she could get through so easily in the night while he was defenseless. He couldn't censor his dreams. Maybe she came every night, had always come every night. Only now, because he was old and slept less soundly, did it awaken him.

Only one image of her was allowed into his conscious memory—a picture, not of her face, but her back as she walked ahead of him on a path through campus. The pleated plaid skirt, navy sweater, and brunette hair bouncing with each step were still vivid. Some days it replayed like an old newsreel as he searched for what he'd seen that had made him brave enough to catch up and introduce himself. What direction would his life have gone if he had not picked that day to skip class and never met her?

He sat up and pulled the chain of the bedside lamp. After dragging an extra pillow behind his back, he reached for a book. He couldn't afford to let his mind wander.

Georgia brought him oatmeal about eight. Her cheeriness was like salt in a fresh wound.

She trumpeted, "Mr. Watts—how was your sleep?" Her voice seemed to match her fatness.

"Auntie, if I thought you gave a crap, I'd tell you." Try as he might, he couldn't get that bubbly smile off her face. When he'd first arrived at Peaceful Meadows, Georgia had ruffled like a wet hen when he called her *Auntie*, but over time she accepted it as an endearing nickname.

Georgia grinned as he choked down the tasteless grain. "Glad to see your appetite is improved this morning, Mr. Watts." He'd probably get a star on his chart out at the nurses' station. If he could report a bowel movement when she checked on him later, he'd have two stars for the day. Success for the remainder of his life would be recorded with stars for eating and crapping.

After she left, he thought about getting up and then thought, *why bother.* He drifted into a nap before being jarred awake by loud voices in the hall. Georgia had left the door open again. The head nurse was introducing a new batch of inmates. All the current residents wandering the halls were being called to "gather 'round."

Barney picked up his novel trying not to listen. The head nurse talked loud for the hearing impaired. He was restarting a paragraph for the third time when he heard the name Crystalina something-or-another. It was such an unusual name, unusual for a white woman anyway. He had to see her, to see if she was black.

By the time he got up and into a bathrobe, the introductions were over. The nurses were escorting the new arrivals to their rooms while current residents ambled away with walkers or canes. It looked like the new crop consisted of two single women and a stoop-shouldered couple walking hand-in-hand. The one black woman in the wheelchair was probably Crystalina. Georgia had the other, a tall, stiffly erect woman, by the elbow walking away toward the west wing. Barney shuffled back to his doorway before taking a second look. The hallway was empty.

Barney usually had lunch alone in his room, but Georgia would knock to invite him to the dining room every day anyway. He waved her in.

"Tell me about the new inmates. That Crystalina woman is colored, right?"

"No, the black lady is Silvia Box. Do you want me to introduce you?"

"No, no. How about the other woman then? What's her name?"

"Crystal Berry. Her name on the application says Crystalina, but she hates that name and wants everybody to call her Crys—"

"Her mother named her Crystal but wanted something more classy on the birth certificate."

"That's what she said! Say, was that a lucky guess or do you know her?"

Barney returned Georgia's stare without comment for a moment before turning to the window. "I've known her all my life."

"You know her? What—?"

"Not feeling well, Auntie. Would you bring me a tray?" He hoped she would get the message and leave.

Barney spent the rest of the afternoon in his overstuffed chair alternately staring out the window and looking back at himself in the dresser mirror. For the first time since puberty, he didn't know what to do.

Even before his daughter Glenda put him in this place, nothing had mattered much. This old-folks home was just the punctuation signifying the end of his story. There had not been a memorable moment when he had stepped aside to let the world go by, but he could trace the beginning back to that night he'd walked away from Crystal. His heart fluttered when he thought her name. Like the memory of her face, the recollection of her name was prohibited also.

This was all so stupid, he knew. These constraints on his memory had once been useful, when he was still determined to forget her, still tempted against all reason to find her again. Even if she were alive, the young vibrant girl of his memory would no longer exist. With all the distortions of age, they wouldn't even recognize each other. What haunted him was the memory of a memory. Why couldn't he just put it behind him, like so many other things?

He studied his face in the mirror. What would she remember? Would the passion that so consumed them once come to mind or the pain of the end? Likely, he would be a mere footnote to her full life. She probably would not be able to place him in the sequence of her lovers.

Barney dressed for the after dinner social hour. There was no sense putting this off. It was part of the routine to get the new arrivals out their first night. The first night was the hardest.

The usual cliques sat in their usual seats playing their usual games. Some played canasta or bridge, while others further down the trail of senility rattled dice in a cup for Chutes and Ladders. The new couple exchanged nervous smiles across a card table by the door; they'd adapt okay. Barney searched the room for the other two. The black woman slumped in her wheelchair, chin resting on her chest as she dozed. Across the table sat Crystal, her head turned away. She either had not noticed him come in or didn't recognize him. Her hair was no longer chestnut but it was cut the same.

"Evening ladies. May I join you?"

Sylvia didn't wake but Crystal turned. The image of the dream this morning flashed as an overlay of her face. The eyes were Crystal's eyes. She stared at him with no hint of recognition, without even a courteous smile. He held to the back of a chair with one hand and looked back through the door. With his free hand, he wiped watery eyes. He wanted to leave, but his legs felt weak and refused to move. She was still staring at him blankly when he turned back to her.

"Would you like some punch?"

Crystal nodded and he shuffled to a table in the middle of the room. Although the attendants called it cocktail hour, the drink was actually fruit juice poured over a block of ice cream. His hands shook as he ladled the soupy concoction into a plastic cup. He craved a drink more than any time since he'd been here. Jack Daniels washed down with beer was the only cure for his palsy. He filled only one cup, not confident he could carry two without spilling. If Sylvia woke up, he'd come back.

He sat the cup before Crystal with both hands, as steadily as he could. She nodded again but still didn't speak. He pulled out a chair, "May I sit?" And then he did before his legs gave out. He looked around the room but every time he came back to her, she had the same perplexed stare. Maybe he looked familiar to her, but she couldn't place him. Maybe she did recognize him but wanted him to go away. Had she hated him all these years?

Another possibility suddenly flushed through him making his shoulders tingle. He leaned toward her, looking deep into her widening eyes. All he saw was confusion. "Crystal?" he called to her. His intensity seemed to scare her and she crouched back in her chair. "Crystal, do you remember?"

One of the attendants from the night shift, alertly watching how the new arrivals were adjusting, was suddenly at her side.

"Ms. Berry, I see you've met Barney. This is Barney Watts, Ms. Berry. There is no need to be afraid of Barney."

Crystal continued to cower, her hands rising to her cheeks.

"He's a nice man, Ms. Berry. Barney won't hurt you."

Barney was on his feet now although he didn't remember getting up. The attendant guided him away from the table with a gentle nudge.

"Maybe Ms. Berry would like a cookie. We've got wonderful chocolate cookies tonight."

At the refreshment table, the attendant put a napkin on Barney's palm and then a cookie. "Mr. Watts, thank you for trying to talk with Crystal. This is her first day at Peaceful Meadows and she's a little frightened. She has trouble remembering things—gets confused. Do you understand?" The attendant continued to hold to Barney's elbow wanting a response. He couldn't talk but nodded.

When he brought the cookie, Crystal's face brightened. The bewilderment on her face before was gone. "Barney," she said with a welcoming smile. The sudden change was disorienting. "Barney," she said again in a lower tone.

He smiled back at the hauntingly familiar voice.

"Would you take me home?"

He dropped the cookie in front of the inert Sylvia and shuffled around to pull back Crystal's chair. She held to his arm as they left. When he turned her up the west wing hallway, she beamed up at him. "I think I'm pregnant, Barney."

Barney remembered this conversation well, the way she had held his arm smiling up at him dreamily. He felt the same constriction in his throat now as he had then.

He opened her door and reached in for the light switch. "That can't be." Was that what he'd said before? He turned his head to the hallway eager to leave.

"Barney, I'm frightened." When he turned back, her eyes had moistened, the eyes from the dream. "Don't leave me, Barney."

He had left her that very night, kissed her that last time at the doorway to her dorm, and walked away. He hadn't thought there was a baby—he'd been careful. And a wife didn't fit into the plans he'd mapped out—to finish school, join the Marines, become an officer, maybe fly jet planes. He'd forget about her soon enough. He hadn't looked back, but she had probably watched him walk away not knowing it was the end.

Some of his plans had come true. Joining the Marine Corps during Viet Nam had been easy enough, but graduating college and the pilot thing didn't happen. There had been other girls, a string of girls. Every girl he chased reminded him of Crystal.

That naïve college boy died at Khe Sanh. Each thud of an incoming mortar being launched mocked the absurdity of trading Crystal's bed for those muddy ditches. While the shell was in flight, he prayed, not for his life or even his soul, but for Crystal's forgiveness. Her apparition squeezed his trembling hand with every explosion. The hope that he might survive to find her again was all that kept him sane.

His mother wrote to him about Crystal's wedding. The Army puke she'd married had deployed to that hellhole also. Her perfumed letters with kisses at the bottom would have been in his helmet—the letters that should have been his.

* * *

Georgia woke him from a sound sleep. "Mr. Watts—you old goat! I've been looking all over the place for you. Get yourself up out'a that bed." Barney sat up, not sure where he was either. "Get these here clothes on, you old goat, and get on out'a here."

"Just hold your horses, Georgia—"

"So, it's Georgia this morning, is it? I ain't your *Auntie* no more? Get yourself up this minute or I'm goin' to call the head nurse in here."

The bed started shaking. Beside him covered by the bedspread, Crystal's body heaved convulsively.

"Look how you shamed her. She won't ever get over this, you old goat."

Barney put his hand on the outline of Crystal's shoulder as it continued to lurch.

"I's goin' for the head nurse. She'll put things right."

"Screw the head nurse, Georgia. We're all over twenty-one here. I ain't leaving her. Go tell that to your head nurse. I ain't ever leaving."

"Well, we'll see about that, you old goat." Georgia put her fists to her hips and glared. "You done took advantage of this poor old woman that don't know nothing." She swirled her skirt and headed for the door. "I'm gonna call your daughter, that's what

I'm gonna do." She spat, "You old goat," one more time before rustling out.

"Screw my daughter too," he yelled after her.

Crystal's shudders seemed more intense and he gave her an apologetic pat on the shoulder. He thought he heard sobs, but when he moved his head closer it didn't sound like crying.

She threw back the cover, reaching out to him, her face beaming a grin. The unreserved joy of a child crinkled her eyes. "You old goat," she taunted while mussing his hair. Giggles from a girl he'd met a long time ago flooded over him.

Lighthouse Mission

Bud walked beside the highway, looking up the side streets as he came to them. Railroad-crossing signs a block over indicated a train track running parallel to the highway. Gallup being the only town for miles, there would be a terminal. An empty boxcar would beat sleeping in the open for the cold desert night. Bud thought about his first train ride just two days before, considering if he wanted to get involved with trains again.

* * *

The freight train passed the boys every day as they walked home from school on the train track. They would lay pennies on the track. Every boy at the orphanage had a cigar box full of squashed pennies. As an engine roared closer, they'd jump in-between the rails forcing the engineer to blast his horn. And as the boxcars swished by, wheels clacking on the rail junctions, they'd inch in on their bellies as close to the massive wheels as they dared.

Then, day before yesterday, while the train was still picking up speed after a stop in town, they ran alongside, keeping pace at a jog. As a prank, for bragging rights, Bud grabbed the ladder on the side of a boxcar and pulled himself up. Looking back, the other boys threw their hands up and cheered his bravado. His plan was to ride out of sight over the next hill, hop off, and beat the other boys home. But the engine accelerated after cresting the hill and he was afraid to jump onto the steep slope of the raised track bed. Not knowing what else to do, he held on, his hands and feet on the ladder rungs, until the train slowed to a stop in a rail yard an hour after dark. He scampered into an open boxcar of a train pulling out the other way—back toward the orphanage.

He rode through the night, finally falling asleep on a stack of cardboard left in the car. Looking out when he awoke, already the hot of the day, he suspected he was far away from Lincoln County, Arkansas. There were no buildings, the hills were gone, and trees were sporadic along far away creek beds. Mature wheat, or fields already harvested and plowed under, stretched to the horizon. Through the day, the landscape became dryer until at nightfall only open prairie could be seen. The train finally stopped in what he later discovered was Raton, New Mexico. A train dick rousted him, chasing him out of the rail yard with vicious curses and a bat.

* * *

Bud cut over to a crossing and followed the rails until they branched into sidetracks at a rail yard. He walked between the boxcars pushing against the doors to see if they would slide. When finally a door screeched open, he looked in both directions, half-expecting to see a train dick running his way. He was boosting himself onto his stomach in the doorway when he heard the crunch of the gravel roadbed behind him and dropped back into a crouch.

"Bad idea," said a dumpy guy in striped coveralls standing at the end of the boxcar.

The man appeared too old to give chase, so Bud didn't immediately start running.

"Might not wake up in the morning if you stay here." The man pulled a red rag from his back pocket and wiped his face "I mean, it would be alright with me, but things happen out here at night." The man squatted with his butt on his heels. "You on your own? Got any money?"

Bud wanted to lie but since one question got a *yes* and one got a *no*, he didn't answer.

"Look," the guy said, "If I was in a strange town and I didn't have no money, and I needed a spot for the night, I think I'd be looking for a mission. There's one not far from here, but you'd better hurry. They don't open their doors after sundown." The man rose and turned so he could point down the track. "Follow this main track for three more crossings then turn to your right for two blocks. It'll be a brown stucco building with a cross over the door."

Bud didn't move, waiting for the man's trick.

"Makes no never-mind to me," the man said. "You're might-near grown and can make up your own mind about things, but that might be your best bet." He turned away and crunched on the crushed stone past the last boxcar and stepped out of sight.

He'll be waiting up there, Bud thought, to jump him when he walks by. He checked the position of the sun, almost down, and zipped up his jacket against the cold.

Where the sidetracks merge back into one, Bud took off at a run past the last boxcar. Glancing back, the guy stood between the rails waving his arm in a wide sweeping arc. Bud ran for a few more paces and then stopped and turned. The man was gone. Bud had wanted to wave back.

The mission looked like it had been a church once and still had a small cross under the roof peak. *Lighthouse Mission* was printed in an arc between the cross and the door. Bud did not know what a mission was exactly, but he thought the cross was a good sign. Knocking lightly, he heard shuffling behind the door and thought he was being watched through the peephole. When the door didn't open, he beat as hard as his knuckles could bear.

The door cracked open and a gaunt face poked through. "What do you want?" When the man spoke, Bud didn't see any teeth. His long nose hooked down almost to his chin.

"I need someplace to go," Bud said. The face continued to study him, then the door opened just wide enough for Bud to slip in.

The man bolting the door wore a long sleeve white shirt buttoned to the top and a narrow black tie. "My name is Brother Randal." The man stood beside a pinch-faced woman in a black dress to her ankles with a white collar clenched around her throat. "This here is Sister Rachael." They both gave him practiced thin-lipped smiles.

"Are you wanting to eat or stay?" the man asked.

Bud didn't know how to answer. "I need a place to sleep—for the night. I ain't asking to live here."

"Now, we've got to ask some questions, just to know if you're a runaway, and then we'll ask you to sign our registry."

Bud told them he was from Arkansas and headed to the Grand Canyon. They didn't seem to like his explanation of how he got here or who his family was. After conferring together out of his hearing, they let him sign a book.

"Sister Rachael will show you the bunkroom."

As he followed her, curiosity got the best of him. "Are you really his sister?"

She glanced sideways and kept walking. "We are brother and sister in Christ." She stopped at an open doorway and stood aside. "Are you a brother?"

Bud imagined he had a sister once, but Rachael was too ugly. "I don't think so."

She waved him in. "Pick any empty bed. The bathroom is this way," she pointed down the hall. "Take a shower right away and come to the kitchen for supper."

"I don't need no shower."

"It's required if you stay here. Need to do it now. We quit serving in ten minutes."

Five cots were in a row with their pillow-ends backed up to the wall. White sheets covered the thin mattresses and folded across the toe end were identical army-surplus green blankets. An Indian stretched out under his blanket on the last bunk, his thick black hair plastered back as if he'd just showered, dark brown eyes staring at the ceiling. Bud threw his coat on the first bunk.

The shower at the orphanage had several showerheads in a cinder-block room. The boys would steam it into a cloud and goose each other. Here it was just a single metal stall with a plastic curtain. The multicolored soap was pressed together cakes of leftover motel soap. His clothes had a sour smell when he put them back on.

Sister served him a bowl of grits and a glass of milk at a picnic table in the kitchen. To the grits, Bud added a pad of butter, two spoonsful of sugar, and covered it over with milk to cool it down.

"Lord bless us and keep us," she prayed. "Help this soul to find its way to you, Lord. Show him the way ... " She went on until the grits got cold. It was more sermon than prayer.

Sister walked him back to the bunkroom. "I'll cut the lights out at nine. Wakeup will be at six. This door stays open. If there's trouble, just call out. We'll hear it," she announced.

The Indian hadn't moved but his eyes were closed. Bud suspected he only pretended to be asleep, awaiting a chance to scalp him. Bud propped himself on a pillow against the wall, his clothes and tennis shoes still on in case he had to run for it.

Next morning, Bud woke to Sister in the doorway clanging a cowbell. "Got to be out in twenty minutes," she yelled in. Still half-asleep, he felt for his hair and was relieved. The Indian, already dressed in blue jeans and a candy-striped shirt with snap buttons, sat on the bed pulling on cowboy boots. Bud followed him to the kitchen.

Sister Rachael brought two bowls of oatmeal and set them on opposite sides of the picnic table. She prayed again before bringing each of them a spoon and a glass of water. Bud bowed his head but kept his eyes on the Indian. After eating, Sister escorted them to the front room where Brother held the door open.

"You both are welcome back; just remember you can't stay here two nights in a row."

Sister handed them both an apple as they walked out. "Have a blessed day."

Bud followed the Indian toward the highway. Ahead, what looked like a dead man lay in the ditch beside the road. The man moaned when the Indian nudged him in the ribs with his pointy-toed boot.

"Mister, are you an Indian or a cowboy?" Bud asked.

The Indian wheeled around with a snarled face, "What do mean by that?"

Bud stepped back out of reach and readied himself to run. "Didn't mean nothing. Just asking."

A grin slowly replaced the scowl. "Boy, I'm an Indian making out like I'm a cowboy. That there … " He pointed to the man in the ditch. "That there is a cowboy making out like he's an Indian."

At the highway, the Indian turned east toward town. When he noticed Bud wasn't following, he stopped and turned. "You headed west? Nothing that way but three hundred miles of desert."

Bud looked down the highway, already quivering with heat. "I reckon I know that."

The List

Vera arrives early to help with the lunch crowd. She stows her purse under the far end of the counter and begins a general appraisal—a backload of unwashed dishes, food waste on the counter and the floor behind. Although she does not look at them directly, she knows the regulars are watching her. It would make these old men uncomfortable to attempt eye contact while they are still checking her out. Later, after they have memorized every wrinkle in her jeans, she'll start to chat.

Jerry works the griddle. A plaintive smile over his shoulder says *another day, same as always.* She accepts this as a good thing and grabs the coffee pot to pour refills. The doorbell tinkles, and in walks Craig. Vera snarls a fake smile, but she's glad to see him. Putting up with his crap will make time go faster.

A hump in his back, not exactly centered, causes Craig to list like a foundering ship. Whether the hump comes from birth, accident, or just age Vera doesn't know. His body faces at an angle to the direction of his walk, so it's never clear where he's headed. Every part of Craig is gnarled. He's worked concrete all his life and still takes small jobs although he looks too old to work. He adjusts himself sidesaddle to a counter stool with one stiff leg off to the side. Craig's usual stool is opposite the sink hidden under the counter. The regulars, out of deference to Craig's appreciation of Vera's breasts, leave this stool for him. Sometimes a woman takes the stool and the regulars think this a waste.

"What's with the pink top?" Craig wants to know.

Vera always wears pink. Today her top is pink imprinted with flowers of various colors, held tentatively just above the nipples with thin straps tied at her shoulders. Underneath, a brown pushup bra makes the pink top look red where the blouse stretches tight. Vera glances *go to hell* as she bends over the sink working down the dishes. The tops of her breasts are puddles that ripple with her slightest movement. Vera knows she makes better tips washing dishes than serving coffee. Jerry claims it's sex discrimination. With tips, Vera pulls in twice as much as him and he does all the work. Once, when working nights, Jerry went a whole shift wearing just an apron. He got nothing extra except a sear on his buttocks when he accidentally backed up to the griddle.

"I think you're trying to convince people you're a girl," Craig says loud enough to get a chuckle out of the regulars.

"Well, I sure hope I am, otherwise I've made a whole lot of mistakes."

Jerry steps back from the griddle and looks approvingly. "I've got faith you're a girl."

"Not me," Craig scoffs, "I need further proof."

Jerry has cooked on day shift off and on for two years now, whenever he is out of jail. He was promoted to days when his predecessor, a cute tease who could also cook, skipped town. There had been a warrant at the request of the VFW where she worked bar after hours. She also stole from the diner, but Bob, the owner, had been too embarrassed to add to the warrant since he had never caught on. Jerry's legal problems are with late child support and drunk driving, nothing that would disqualify him for flipping burgers. After talking with the regulars, Bob had concluded Jerry is honest. Since the cash register is against the back wall in plain view of the counter, they'd known about the prior cook, but never said anything until after she left town. Stealing is one thing but ratting out your friends leads to a bad reputation.

Unable to get a rise out of Vera, Craig turns to Jerry. "Back from vacation, I see. How were the city's accommodations?"

"Great," Jerry cracks back over his shoulder as he flips an egg, "relaxing—slept most of the time."

"Expensive?"

"Not really. It's one of those all-inclusives, you know. Toward the end they wanted everything I could borrow, to let me out. I took an advance from Bob, so now I'm working for nothing."

"Saw in the paper some guy hanged himself out there yesterday," Craig recalls. "Tore up a sheet and hanged himself from a bunk bed. You got to really want to kill yourself to hang yourself from a bunk bed."

"I can lay my arms on the top bunk." Jerry holds out his arms parallel to the floor to show how high.

Craig rubs his neck with one hand, "It would just be strangling yourself. After trying that a while, I think I'd have to give it up and say, 'hey, I'll do this another day'." Craig admires the grit of a man who is clear about what he wants and does what it takes to get it.

There's a hocking behind Craig, like a gob of tobacco is about to hit the floor. Craig spins on his stool to see Sammy bent to some task hidden under his massive paws. "What you working on?"

Sammy does not sit at the counter with the other regulars because he takes up too much room. In addition to the counter stools, there are two tables against the wall. His spot is at the table by the door that is never used. When he arrives, he moves two chairs side-by-side and spreads out. Today, he is processing a quart basket of strawberries into a glass dish. He cuts the stems off with a small paring knife he borrowed from Jerry.

"A strawberry milkshake. Here, you want to try some?" He extends the basket at Craig. "They're really sweet. Got a deal from this Mennonite. Some of them are overripe, but they're still good, except for a few that have a whang." Not wanting to risk his milkshake, he sorts out the bad ones as he goes by eating anything questionable. The spoiled ones, he spits it onto a paper napkin.

With all the berries in the bowl, he sprinkles on sugar from the little packets at the table and brings the bowl to Jerry at the counter. "Put about half in the shake and the rest is for you. Don't use any of that flavored syrup, it's got artificial sugar."

Sammy's life is dedicated to food. He spends most of his disability money on burgers and milkshakes at the diner. When that runs out toward the end of the month, he just watches everybody else eat. He takes great interest in everything being served and cranes up to look over the counter when he hears sizzling from the griddle. His nose rises to taste the air like a discerning beagle before he settles back with the vacuous grin of a drunk at a titty bar.

Jerry dumps half the berries along with scoops of ice cream into the stainless cup of the antique milkshake machine. The shafts of the mixing tines are black from dried residue. When he turns it on, there is an encouraging whir, but then the berries bog it down and Jerry rushes back from the griddle to make adjustments before it stalls out.

The regulars, one by one, decline the rest of the berries. Jerry scoots the bowl in front on Ruby when she walks in and sits beside Craig for her morning coffee. Dark smoke from Ruby's cigarillo momentarily hangs in front of her glasses as she takes a drag and contemplates the pink glob. One can imagine she had been a looker in a previous era. There is a tattoo of the tail of a dragon on Ruby's right calf. The blue outline of the dragon continues up her thigh with the stubby front paws reaching up into her shorts. The dragon's head is speculated to be at the joining of her legs. None of these old men claim to know for sure.

"There she go-o-oes!" Ruby cries out as if she's spotted a whale. Jerry, his spatula clanging to the griddle, pivots instantly to the diner's front window. Across the street, a seductively dressed mother with a youngster in tow is en route to the courthouse. "Not much ass or tits," Ruby apologizes.

Craig has already made his appraisal. "With Jerry's imagination, she don't need much."

Ruby is sympathetic to the appetites of the old men. And she doesn't see she's doing a disservice to the women walking by. They don't buy those skimpy dresses for nothing. Vera knows Ruby would rather be the young woman getting stripped naked by the gawkers.

"If you can't fish; cut bait," Ruby says to Craig's sideways glance.

Craig slaps the counter. "Jerry, that popcorn machine has got to go." The commercial popper with the tall glass enclosure and a tipping-bowl in the center obstructs nearly a third of the picture window.

"It would add to my job satisfaction," Jerry, still looking across the street, agrees.

The popper has been prominently displayed in this exact location for two years, since Bob bought it at an auction. At the next street festival, there were lines out the door for popcorn. But after filling up on popcorn, nobody wanted a sandwich. And Jerry was too busy filling bags with popcorn to cook anyway. The popper persists in the window, unpopped kernels in the bottom, oil streaking the inside of the glass, untouched since that festival.

When Bob's truck pulls up outside, Jerry turns from the griddle to wink at Craig. "You talk to him." He knows Craig won't say anything because mention of the popper would lead to Bob's endless justification for buying it. It might actually lead to renewed use of the popper, which stinks up the whole joint.

Bob unloads several crates of vegetables and starts arranging the display in front of the picture window. In addition to the produce, the folding table contains an assortment of birdhouses and other deals he's run across.

"How was that cantaloupe?" Jerry asks. Craig bought one a few days ago.

"Rotten."

"Well, get you another one." Jerry waves to the pile just outside the window.

"Did that yesterday. They're all rotten. I'll wait until he gets a new load and try one then." Bob buys low at the farmers market at closing time after every thing's been picked over. The sweet corn especially attracts flies that slip in with every customer. Vera keeps a fly swatter on the counter for anybody's use.

Some regulars will not come in if they see Bob's red truck out front. There is no specific reason customers are uncomfortable around Bob, except for his sense of humor. When not out finding bargains, he sits at the counter, empty stools on each side, the usual banter going on around him. Occasionally a barb is directed his way. His reaction is always a startled *what was that?* as he cups his good ear with a hand. During the explanation of the joke, Bob scrunches up his nose to lift his thick glasses and tilts his head back to get additional magnification. Looking up his flared nostrils is the penalty for taking a jab at Bob. The pupils of his eyes behind the coke-bottle glasses are like big black bugs struggling in slime. So dizzying is the effect, Vera grabs the counter with both hands when she talks with Bob.

When Bob finally walks in, Craig waves him over to the stool next to him. Behind Bob, Vera can see Jerry's headshake *no,* pleading with Craig not to mention the popper.

"Bob, that's got to go," Craig says.

"What was that?" Bob replies cupping his ear. Behind, Jerry makes praying hands, his mouth in a silent cry.

Craig points above the register. "It gives me the creeps every time I come in here. It creeps everybody out. I check every time I come in here to see if my name's up there yet."

Beside the lighted menu sign is a list of names printed on the wall in black. The last names toward the bottom are freshly painted, but the others are muted under layers of grease and tobacco smoke stain. Bob slumps on the stool, his face turned down to the counter. Vera knows he wants the list gone too. Once he came in with paint and roller, but the regulars threw a fit. *These were real people,* they had argued. *For some, it would be erasing the only proof they ever existed. You may rent this building, but that don't give you the right to just paint over people.*

Nobody knows when the list started. Probably some regular printed his dead friend's name up there as a tribute and then that guy's name was added below it when he died. There were already over twenty names when Vera started here five years ago. People could ignore the list except new names keep getting added. A name would just be there one day and nobody would own up to writing it. Bob fired Jerry the last time it happened but begged him back when the regulars vowed his innocence.

* * *

The following morning, Vera watches Jerry rummage in the closet at the back end of the diner. He comes out with an empty pickle jar with a paper label taped to the side. As Jerry walks to the counter, he checks the name on the label against the list on the wall. He sets the jar on the counter in front of Craig, peels off the label, wads it up, and drops it in the trash before turning to the register. After a moment he comes back with a card from the back of an order-pad, Scotch tape, and the marker used to write on the Styrofoam to-go boxes.

"I ain't doing it," Craig declares pushing it all down the counter in front of the next stool.

"Come on Craig, you know he didn't have no relatives. Ain't nobody going to bury him if we don't."

"It ain't the collection. I'll put mine in like everybody else. But just why do you think it ought to be me that writes his name on there?" Craig is in a pissy mood.

"He'd do it for you. You know he'd give you anything he had, he just never had nothing."

When the bell tinkles, nobody turns. Ruby takes a couple of steps in and stops when she sees Craig intently examining the list and the pickle jar beside him.

"Who?" Ruby settles on the stool beside Craig. He doesn't seem to hear her.

"Sammy," Jerry finally answers. "Dropped dead on his walk home yesterday."

Ruby turns to the table by the door. She wouldn't have noticed when she walked in if Sammy had been sitting there or not. He was like the wallpaper.

"Dropped dead, just like that," Vera says. "People should linger at the point of death at the hospital for a while first. Gives people time to get useta the idea." Vera thinks Sammy was a slob anyway, so who cares. She spins the card and picks up the marker. "What was his last name anyway?"

"Blatto. B-L-A-T-T-O." Craig wants to help now. He wouldn't have known Sammy's last name either unless he had inquired at the courthouse earlier.

"B-L-A-T-T-O," Vera repeats as she writes. "He looked like a Blatto." Jerry turns to glare and she returns a *whatever* with the shrug of her shoulders.

Bob's truck pulls to the curb out front. He examines the produce display and makes adjustments before coming in. "Sammy's dead," he announces. Nobody turns or looks up. Bob can't see well enough to discern facial expressions and is not perceptive enough to know what they meant if he could. With his hearing aid, he can never tell how loud he's talking so he yells, "Sammy's dead!"

Craig's head turns toward Bob, but his eyes stay on the list. "Heard it already, Bob. Got a jar started. We'll call the funeral home when we get enough for a deposit."

Bob walks around the counter, leans on the cash register, pointing at the list. "I don't want nobody back here, Jerry, do you hear me. Nobody comes back here."

"I've got to run the till," Jerry explains.

"Nobody but you. Understand?"

"And who's gonna watch you?" Craig says.

Bob puffs up. He rocks his head back and scrunches up his nose as he looks at them one at a time. They all support Craig. "Nobody watches me. This is my place."

"Well, I think somebody should and I think I'll appoint me," Craig says.

"And I think you need to get the hell out of here."

"And I think this is a public place and I plan to be here anytime you are."

"It's misspelled," Ruby whispers to herself, squinting at the wall. Craig and Bob are about to continue their bluster but pull up. If Vera had yelled "fire" at the top of her lungs they wouldn't have noticed, but they got quiet to hear what Ruby had to say. "The last name on the list, Riddle, is misspelled. Whoever wrote it on the wall misspelled it."

"Get out of the way, Bob," Craig orders. Bob stands right in front of the list, his mouth still open, slow to catch on as usual.

Jerry comes over so he can see too. "It ain't misspelled. It's just the same way it was spelled on the jar—Tom Riddel." As they watch, he pulls out the trashcan and starts digging. He shakes the coffee grounds off a wad of paper and spreads it on the counter. "See. Tom R-I-D-D-E-L, just like on the wall."

"Well, that was his name then," Bob explains.

"Riddle is not spelled that way. There is no Riddle spelled R-I-D-D-E-L. Look in the phone book," Ruby says.

Nobody considers looking in the phonebook. Craig went to school with Ruby when they were growing up. She went to Vanderbilt on scholarship whereas Craig couldn't get out of the eleventh grade. Ruby was a teacher at Franklin High for a while before she got into it with some mouthy senior. Punched him out according to Craig.

"Nah," Jerry says, "his name really was spelled that way. It was Tom's daddy that couldn't spell. He told me the story how he couldn't get into the VA hospital because they couldn't find his records. When he enlisted, they corrected his name. But on his birth certificate, it was spelled the other way.

Everybody glares at Jerry. "Who else knows that story?" Craig asks.

Jerry tries to look innocent. "Now wait a minute. I can see where this is going." He turns and stomps past the griddle up to the front window and stares out sulking. And then, as if struck by a hammer, he bends over and grabs his knees. He rushes back to the register, but seeing their startled faces, he bends over laughing again. He holds his breath and pounds the counter in an effort to stop sniggering. His voice goes high under the strain of talking and laughing at the same time. "Well, you can think again. I was doing thirty days for contempt of court when Tom died. When his name went on the wall I was in lockup and I've got court papers to prove it."

Craig's mouth forms a little 'O' like a startled monkey. He settles back on the bar stool suddenly remembering his coffee is cold and holding up his cup up for Vera to see. Bob returns to the customer side of the counter and hikes onto a stool two down from Craig. As Vera does the warm-ups, Jerry cuts her a sly glance. Her lips silently form the word *asshole*, knowing he's behind it all somehow.

Everybody avoids looking at the list or each other. But after a few minutes, Ruby goes behind the counter for a closer look. A yellowed typing paper sign advertising a pork chop special for $7.99 is immediately under the last name. With her fingernails, she scrapes at the tape at the bottom corners. She lifts the paper for only a glance and then tapes it back. All eyes follow her as she walks to the front window, squinting as if there's something in the street she can't quite make out.

"This is the oldest building in town." Ruby speaks distinctly but to no one in particular, like she's thinking out loud. She looks back at the room but doesn't seem to notice them raptly staring at her. "This place was a dress store until it was remodeled into a diner in the 1930s. That's when it happened, I think. It could have been the whittler's bench under the oaks at the courthouse or the barbershop at the corner, but when you think about it, it had to be here. This diner is where the country folks have always come to catch up on news since their last town-visit. They picked up their gossip here like they picked up their staples from the stores around the square. Every person that's lived in the county over the last eighty years has been in here at one time or another. This place has known us all."

Without looking at anyone, she comes back to the counter, picks up her slouch purse, and heads for the door. Everyone watches as the doorbell tinkles and she speeds past the window without looking in. Bob and Craig stare at each other. And then, as if signaled with a gunshot, they rush behind the counter from opposite ends. Bob struggles to scrape up the tape with his thumbnail until Craig snatches the paper off in a wad.

"It wasn't me," Jerry declares. "I quit. I've had enough of this crap." He throws the spatula at a burger now burning on the griddle and stomps out.

Bob wanders to the picture window but his eyes are not following Jerry who has a short fuse and will be back later begging for his job. He's trying to see what Ruby saw. He is startled when he notices Craig at his elbow.

"I'm taking up drinking again," Craig says. "I can figure things better when I'm drinking." Craig stands beside Bob for a moment, both looking out into the street before he says, "See you later." As the door tinkles, he adds, "Or maybe not."

Bob walks back past the griddle, raking the burnt burger in the trash, on to the register where Vera is studying the list. Under Sammy's name is a dark smudge, an inky palm print left by whoever wrote Sammy's name on the wall—or maybe a new name starting to form itself.

Grand Canyon

A woman standing beside the highway in a party dress and high heels, metallic beads gleaming at her neck, reminded Bud of his mother. As he walked toward her, she became less pretty, hair disheveled, makeup smeared. She watched apprehensively as he approached and then as he walked past, she broke into a warm smile.

"Good morning young fellow, where you headed?"

"Grand Canyon."

She pursed her smudged lips and ratcheted back her head to squint at the sky like she was working on a riddle. "Do you even know where it is? It's like a long way from here—way up north."

"I reckon I know where it is or I wouldn't be goin'," Bud said tersely.

"Well, I'm headed back to Flagstaff. Hope I'm headed in the right direction. This is Gallup, right?"

When Bud kept walking, she tried to follow, but her high heels dug into the sand causing her to lurch. She tippy-toed onto the edge of the pavement and caught up to him.

"The two of us should stick together. More likely people will stop for a mother and child than for either of us by ourselves. Don't remember getting here, really. Met this fellow at a party— Freddie, I think it was. Nice dresser and generous, too. This morning, woke to someone beating on the door of my room at that motel back there." She pointed behind Bud. "Never seen him before, motel manager or something. Says I passed him some counterfeit money. Told him I didn't give him nothing, to talk to Freddie about it. But Freddie wasn't around, so he ... "

Suddenly her mouth flew open like somebody poked her in the ribs. She threw her floppy handbag in the sand and fell to her knees, rummaging inside until she pulled out a wad of money. She stretched two $100 bills against her knee.

She thrust them at Bud. "Are these real?" and then she held them up to the sun one at a time. "That son of a bitch. I'll cut his nuts off if he ever comes through Flagstaff again." She looked fierce like she could do it, not like his mother anymore. But then she slumped back onto her butt, covered her face with her hands. Her shoulders bounced as she sobbed. Bud stepped closer with the urge to touch her hair, console her someway, but stopped short with the memory of that savage face. And that's the way he left her, with her legs crumpled under the yellow-flowered dress with only the red shoes sticking out like the fruit of some tropical bush.

Past the last building in Gallup, where the desert began again, a faded pickup slowed and stopped ahead of him without him even putting out his thumb. He ran to catch up and started crawling into the bed. An arm out the passenger side window motioned for him to get in the cab instead. A squat woman got out and let him in the middle to ride the hump. The driver, a leather-skinned man wearing a cowboy hat, asked something in Indian. When Bud answered "Grand Canyon," the man looked at the woman and chuckled.

In the center of the dashboard, mounted on a spring, a plastic statue of the Virgin Mary bowed back and forth as the man went through the gears. As the day wore on, Bud shut his eyes against the sun's glare and dozed, waking with a start when his head fell against the squaw's breast. She smiled reassuringly, gently pushing his head against the seatback.

The desert became a black void beyond the blare of headlights. Backlit by the dash's glow, The Virgin Mary, pink arms outstretched from underneath her painted blue robe, beckoned him closer, like she had secrets to tell.

The Collector

I found Jimbo a few weeks back and I've been coming to this diner for breakfast ever since. He's always here. I buy him a honeybun, breakfast of champions he calls it, and we talk—or rather I listen. Sometimes I have to ask him a question to prime the pump, but get him going and you never know what stories he'll come up with. He's going to be a character in this book I'm writing.

I try to entice him over to the counter, but he's too excited for breakfast this morning. The owner has hung a replica antique phone on the wall between the silkscreen Elvis and the jukebox.

"See my new phone? It's a direct line to Elvis." Jimbo puts the receiver to his ear, smiling as he pretends to listen. The smile fades to concentration as he looks blankly out the café's glass front. His head nods slowly, his mouth opening like he wants to say something but doesn't want to interrupt. He lays the receiver on the table and asks me, "Want to hear some music? Want to play the jukebox?"

I want to see where this is going so I give him a dollar in quarters. He studies the front of the jukebox with a coin poised looking for where it goes. He feeds in the quarters and then seems puzzled about how to make a selection. Finally, a guitar riff begins followed by a mellow bass voice: —*sixteen tons, what do you get ... Saint Peter don't you call me 'cause I can't go*—. Jimbo adjusts the phone receiver on the table to face the jukebox so Elvis can hear.

Before he got shot, Jimbo had been a guitar session player for the Nashville studios. If I get him talking about the old days, he mentions Chet and Hank, not name-dropping, just stories about some old buddies. Occasionally, out of nowhere, to the delight of the regulars, he'll break out in a stanza of some old Opry standard. I'm satisfied he knows every word to every country song prior to 1970.

Now, Jimbo's job is to do warm-ups on the coffee in exchange for an occasional hamburger. When prompted for a warm-up, he'll shuffle off in a hurry toward the coffee pot, but he's likely to bring back some packets of sugar or hot sauce. When his brain put itself back together after the bullet, a lot of wires got crossed.

While I'm studying Jimbo, an old black man, skinny, kinky beard—mostly white, comes in tiptoeing as if on hot coals. He sneaks onto a stool on the other side of the counter from Vera whose back is turned making coffee. His wide flat nose sits atop the mischievous grin on his thick purple lips.

"Come in here to give youse some trouble," he says to Vera when she turns. He continues an indistinct babble mixed with short laughs.

"You ain't causing me no trouble, old man. I can talk loony too," is Vera's surly reply. I can tell from Vera that he's been in before, but I've never seen him.

"You's my adversity. I's gonna gets you one day," he says and laughs. You can't hear the laugh, but you can tell from the way his head bobs that he's laughing. Vera rolls her eyes with an exasperated *whatever* expression before scurrying away to clean a table.

As the old man's eyes follow Vera, he spots me two stools down staring at him. "Seen you before, Mister. You from some agency, ain't ye?"

A pink tongue circles his lips as he awaits my reply. Despite the maniacal gleam in his eyes, I figure he's just a harmless halfwit. I should ignore him, turn away, but he's like a turtle I've found that I've got to turn on its back.

"I've been following you around," I say. "People say you act insane so you can get a disability check."

"Don't need none of that. I's sixty-five. I gets my gov'ment check without no foolishness." He turns away like his feelings are hurt and then his head whips back around, "North Dakota. Seen you in North Dakota."

My older brother lives in North Dakota, but I've never been there.

"Ever been to North Dakota?" I ask.

"Nope, always been right here 'cept in the Navy."

"Then you didn't see me in North Dakota, did you?"

He laughs into the crook of his arm "Not yet I ain't. People thinks I's crazy cause I sees things."

"What sort of things?"

"Oh, just things. Sometimes in da future, sometimes in da past."

"Well, what do you see?"

"Accidents fore da happen, stuff like dat." He is quiet a moment studying my face. "Where's you from? You not from here. Not ridge'nally."

"Mississippi, way back," I say.

"Jackson … " he sees my head begin to shake. "Tupelo. You from Tupelo. Got two sons," he studies my face, "and a daughter. You got two sons and a daughter—and a granddaughter, too."

"You're close. You're right on Tupelo and the two sons." He's good, I'm thinking, probably been hustling people with this sort of stuff all his life.

"Offsprings. You knows, that's the number offsprings you got." He screws up his face like I'm too dumb to understand. He swivels on the stool and smiles wide, "Hey, Jimbo."

Jimbo, still minding the phone for Elvis, points to the earpiece and then puts his pointer finger to his lips to shush the old man while Elvis is talking.

The old man pivots back to face me, "You knows Jimbo?" he asks. "Ever talks with Jimbo? Some people thinks other people's a fool. But Jimbo, he knows things."

"Yeah, it's scary the stuff he knows. Might not remember breakfast, but he remembers fifty years ago like a picture—every detail."

"Hey, Jimbo," I yell over, "how'd Elvis get his start anyway?" I want to show off Jimbo.

Jimbo hesitates, looking down at the table pretending to be thinking, but he already knows the answer. "Well, let's see. He got his first guitar for his eleventh birthday. He wanted a .22 rifle, but his momma said no, so he settled for a guitar. If he'd got the gun, nobody woulda ever heard of him." He puts the phone receiver to his ear and listens while his eyes dance around the room. "Yep, that was it," he reports.

Vera sets coffee on the counter in front of the black man, then scoots away before he can start with the babble. As he looks down in the cup, his smile drains away like his mind has wandered somewhere else.

"Must be tough seeing stuff other people don't see," I say trying to keep our conversation going.

"People thinks I's crazy. Cause they can't see what I see, they's think *I's* the crazy one. Black-folks is scared of me; thinks I'm a demon. But I was called to be a preacher when just a boy."

"So why aren't you a preacher?"

"Coulda took advantage cause what I knowd; the Devil would've tempted me."

"So, the Devil was close too?"

"Yeah, he close. He always close. And he strong too, stronger'n God-Almighty, sometimes. Makes you do bad things; claims your soul."

A prodding in my brain finally breaks through, causing my scalp to tingle. When he sees my face change, he jerks back like he's expecting to get hit. "There *IS* a daughter!" I say behind clenched teeth. "By my best friend's wife!" I glance around the room; Vera's giving me a startled look. Scooting over to the stool beside the old man, I lean in close and whisper, "How'd you know that? Nobody knows that but me and her." His smile is returning when it occurs to me, "And my daughter's got a daughter; that's the granddaughter."

His mouth eases open in a grin showing the stubs of two tarnished teeth, "I reckon that's so." His eyes gleam as his head bobs with a chuckle.

I reach for my wallet, putting a five on the counter for the coffee. I've got to get away.

"You's collects people, don't ye?" he says.

"What you mean by that?" I feel like choking him, reaching through the beard, and grabbing that scrawny neck before he can answer.

"Naw, naw, just talking, making conve'sation. No cause to get riled. You's collected Jimbo already and I can feel you collecting me." His friendly smile turns into a sly grin that stops my breath. "Well, I's a collector too."

He turns on his stool back to the counter, catching Vera's attention. "I's going to get ye," he tells her, his head bobbing in that silent laugh. He's through with me—like I've been folded up and stuffed in the bib of his overalls to be played with later like some character in a story.